Crackscam

by

Tony Stowell

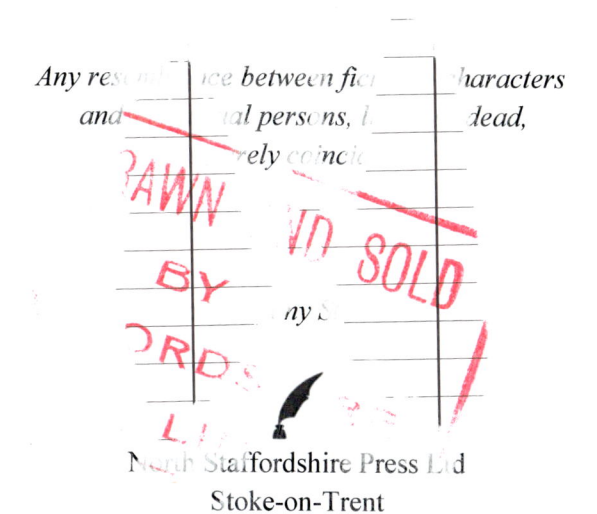

Any resemblance between fictional characters and actual persons, living or dead, is purely coincidental.

North Staffordshire Press Ltd
Stoke-on-Trent
Staffordshire

Crackscam

All Rights Reserved

No part of this book may be reproduced in any form by photocopying or any electronic or mechanical means, including information storage and retrieval systems, without permission in writing from both the copyright owner and the publisher of this book.

ISBN 978-0-9568198-5-7

First Published in 2012
By
North Staffordshire Press
Staffordshire University Business Village
72 Leek Road, Stoke-on-Trent, Staffordshire
United Kingdom

Printed and bound by Design Bindings Ltd, Staffordshire

The Author

Tony Stowell was born in Surrey, and educated at Caterham School. After being commissioned in the RAF, he graduated from Cambridge with an MA in History, to which he later added an MSc from Oxford in Educational Planning and Administration. He retired early from the world of education, and he and his wife Rosalind have since been engaged in local affairs in the Cotswold town where he now lives, being Mayor for 2001-2003, and acting as an advice worker for the Citizens Advice Bureau.

He is Chairman of the Cotswold Writers Circle. He has written two full length novels, one a light thriller, The Woolsack Conspiracy, and one much more serious book about education, A Little Learning. He also writes poems, many of which have been published locally. His poetry has been read on Poetry Please on Radio 4

He is a practised public speaker, and has appeared on local television and radio.

Dedicated to my wife Ros ~
for putting up with long periods of absence or introspection,
with thanks to Rob Dickenson for doing the proof-reading and the
Cotswold Writers Circle for their interest and input.

Chapter 1

I woke up with a start. Someone was in my bedroom.

I lay motionless, fearing the violent beating of my heart might arouse the suspicion of the figure at the bottom of my bed. Wide-eyed, I tried to see as much of him as I could without moving my head.

The street lamps filtered through the curtains and threw a dull light on the unfamiliar room. The intruder was investigating the dressing table facing my bed.

What could a burglar want? I was staying in the company overnight room after working late on a project. I had nothing of importance, no company secrets or sensitive industrial documents, only a few personal items like credit cards – certainly nothing worth breaking in for.

What the hell was I to do? The intruder didn't seem to realise I was there, or at least was at pains to let me sleep on, as he methodically went through my belongings, examining each item with a pencil torch which he carefully shielded with his hand. He made almost no sound.

He was dressed in a sort of black spider-man outfit which suggested that he was a professional. On the other hand he was only five foot five or six, slim build. It was worth having a go, partly because I was outraged that he should invade my bedroom, and partly because I fancied my chances. I am five eleven, thirteen stone, and the Wednesday evening training sessions at the rugby club would stand me in good stead.

I also had the advantage of surprise. I lay under a thin duvet, which was good, but I had nothing else on, which was not so good. Whatever, I decided to sort him out.

When he appeared to be about to open the second drawer, I leapt forward off the bed holding the corners of the duvet, which I wrapped squarely over his head and shoulders. I reckoned I had got him.

I reckoned wrong. He somehow wriggled round and brought his knee sharply up into my groin. I groaned out loud at the intense sudden pain, and let go of the duvet, falling backwards onto the bed. He struggled free from the enveloping cloth and made a leap for the door.

In sheer desperation, I kicked out as he went, and had the satisfaction of catching his ankle in mid-air. Hopelessly off-balance, he crashed to the ground, his head catching the corner of the dressing-table with a gratifying thud.

Staggering off the bed, I felt I had regained some advantage. He was lying face-down on the carpet, motionless, outlined by the light of his torch. He was out cold.

He might come round at any moment so I had to act fast to be sure he could make no more trouble. In the dim light I urgently rummaged in my brief-case for a roll of sellotape and taped him up. Arms behind the back; thumbs together first, which I remembered from somewhere, then palms separately. Next, bind the legs with several rounds of tape, and finally bend the knees back and secure the ankles to the wrists. There was no way anyone can get out of that, so I could relax.

Panting from my exertions, I stood up and switched on the bedside light. I wanted to see who this joker was. He was enveloped in a black ski suit, which I supposed all professional thieves might consider appropriate wear. He was not as big as I had imagined.

I pulled back his hood. A mass of blond locks tumbled out on to the floor. Bloody hell, it was a girl, a young woman.

Then I realised who she was – she had been spending the last couple of weeks auditing the company accounts. So what the hell was she doing burgling my bedroom in the middle of the night dressed like a strip cartoon?

She showed signs of coming round, and it suddenly occurred to me that, after all the excitement, I was still stark naked.

I thought I'd better put some clothes on. I pulled on my jeans and a sweat-shirt, and was thrusting my feet into my trainers when she regained her senses.

There was a look of bewilderment on her face, followed by fear, then despair, then anger when she realised she was taped up. I almost felt sorry for her.

"Hello," I said lamely.

She focussed on me for the first time, and seemed to relax a little.

"But you're, er…" she muttered, perplexed.

"Yes," I replied, "Oliver Howson, the production engineer. I've seen you doing the audit. I'm sorry, I don't know your name."

"Emma. Emma Crawford."

She had turned ashen white, and perspiration beaded her forehead. "For God's sake, get me out of this."

"Well, Emma, I rather think you have some explaining to do."

"Just get me out of this," she said, panic rising in her voice. "Please."

I looked at her, and she appeared pretty pathetic. Pretty and pathetic, in fact. I wondered if I was wise to release her without an explanation which would satisfy me, and felt that she would have to be unusually inventive to come up with a convincing story. But she was in no position to make a getaway, and the least I could do was to hear her out. I only hoped she would make it plausible.

I found some scissors and carefully removed all the hastily applied tape.

"Thanks," she said. "Do you by any chance have an aspirin? My head aches."

"Yes and I think I'll join you. I've got a couple of aches myself."

She grinned ruefully. "Sorry."

"Where did you learn a trick like that?"

"At college. There were a number of attacks on female students, and we all attended self defence courses."

"You learnt very well."

"You took me by surprise. I had no idea you were there."

I gave her a glass of water to wash the pill down, and felt that it was time for the serious bit. What the hell was she doing there?

She read my thoughts. She deliberated for a few moments before speaking.

"What am I doing here? Well, I'm going to have to trust you, and hope you are not in it with them."

"Try me," I said, intrigued.

"Well, as you know, I have been doing the annual audit for the Company. Everything seemed to be fine. Your chief accountant has everything in apple pie order, completely correct. A model of accounting practice."

I could understand that. Linus McEwan was almost a caricature of an accountant, accurate, humourless, as precise with words as he was with figures. I imagined he had very little social life, being in his fifties and unmarried, and was not what you would call a social being. He lived to a predictable regime with no fripperies. Mistakes did not feature in his world, nor trivia.

"What is the problem, then? It must make your work easy."

"It should have done. All the accounts are computerised, and I've seen the figures. It was just that…." she tailed off, puzzled.

"Out with it," I encouraged.

"Well I went up to his office for a final check on a couple of small points, and he was engrossed in his computer screen. He suddenly jumped up and cursed. He had been stung in the neck by an early wasp. He was in a panic, and shouted that he was allergic to wasps, and rushed out to get some antihistamine from the medical cabinet.

"While he was out, I glanced at his screen – and couldn't believe my eyes. There was the company account, headed by the company logo, and it was quite different from what I had been working on."

"How different?" I asked.

"What would you expect the annual turnover to be?" she asked after a pause.

"Don't know exactly. We have been doing quite well recently. Something over one and a half a million, perhaps two million pounds."

"Quite, that is what my figures said. But this account had a bottom line of over fifteen million."

There was a pause while I took this in.

"Fifteen million? You've got to be joking!"

Her eyes flashed defiance.

"Look, I've told you. What is it about fifteen million pounds that you don't understand?" Her indignation couldn't have been clearer.

"Sorry, but it can't be true."

"Of course it isn't. I was gobsmacked. Anyway, I had a quick second look, and then heard him coming back. He was swelling up horribly around the neck, and was beginning to come out in blotches. He said he had to get to hospital, so I ran to the office to get someone to drive him there. He cleared up and followed me down. I later heard that he had been kept in overnight for observation."

"Yes, we were quite concerned. People can die of wasp stings."

"Those figures bothered me. At the end of the afternoon, I had a look in his office. I had noticed he had not been using a memory stick, but no accountant would ever deal with that sort of information without backing it up, so he must have been using a compact disc. I had a good look, but couldn't find anything that looked suspicious. When I got home, I spent a long time thinking what I should do. This is important to me. I'm a trainee accountant, on a graduate conversion course, and this is the first time I've handled a full audit on my own. I was given this account because it was thought to be completely unproblematic. However, there was something seriously wrong with those figures, and I was just about to sign them off as accurate. I couldn't get it out of my mind. There was no way I could sign off the audit without having some explanation, especially as they had been deliberately concealed from me. I had to check them. Then I remembered that Linus stayed in this room last night."

"Yes, some of us do that if we are working late. That's why I'm here tonight. That, and the fact that my car is at the garage having a paint job done on the wing."

"I thought that he wouldn't have taken the disc to hospital so I snuck back to look for it. It wasn't in his office, so I thought it might be here. I'd no idea someone else was in the room."

"Why all the cat-woman outfit? I really thought you were a professional sneak-thief."

"I know. It's silly really, but I only had my light spring coloured clothes with me. I felt that although I had a legitimate master key, I didn't wish to be seen swanning around in the middle of the night making myself obvious. I put on the only dark clothes I had, which was the ski wear I brought back from holiday a couple of weeks ago. I felt a real idiot at the gate, and had to wait until the guard went on his rounds before I got through. It was easy once I was inside."

I had to admit she fitted into her ski suit very well as she looked earnestly at me, wondering if I would believe her extraordinary story.

Frankly, I had my doubts, though I acknowledged to myself that she had come up with a more convincing explanation than I had expected.

"What do you think we should do about it?" I asked, hoping to throw the responsibility back to her.

"I don't know. I've no way of coming to any sensible conclusion, unless I have a proper look at that disc. For all I know it might just be an advanced computer game. It is the sort of nerdish thing that some people get up to. But I don't think so in this case. The figures looked too realistic. What's more, I don't think Linus is the sort of person who would play those games."

I could only agree with that analysis.

"How good a look did you get at his office earlier?" I enquired

"Well, reasonable, but not as thorough as I would have liked."

I still didn't fully believe her story, but thought it was worth taking her at her word. If I suggested going through the office again, and we found the disc, it would corroborate her explanation. If we didn't find it – well, we'd come to that later.

"Why don't we both go to his office now? It's only downstairs and along the corridor, and at least we won't be disturbed. If it's there, we'll find it, and you can have a chance to look at it properly. You can use my computer if you wish."

She agreed unhesitatingly, and we moved off somewhat gingerly as she was still a bit shaky, and so was I. We found Linus' office in immaculate order, and we spent half an hour in a detailed search. All the discs were neatly lined up and correctly labelled, and each one was exactly what it said. There were no discrepancies.

We searched every possible hiding place, but finally had to admit to ourselves that wherever the disc was, it was not in there.

Defeated, we returned to my room. I made Emma a cup of coffee, and we sat on the bed and decided what to do next.

"I can't ignore what I saw," said Emma seriously. "I just don't know what to do."

"No, I can see you have a problem," I commented. "You can hardly go to him and say, 'Can I see your dodgy disc?' – can you? But what I don't see is what the disc could be doing. Linus is about the most upright citizen I know."

"That's what I felt. On the other hand, respectability is the best disguise for anyone up to some financial fiddle. You would be surprised what we see in some of our auditing work. This alternative account either means some scam is running on the side, with or without the company's knowledge, or an unofficial money-laundering operation. It's impossible to tell. All I know is that millions of pounds are being handled secretly under the company's name. This looks like a serious criminal activity, and one which could be disastrous for the company and Linus must know about it."

Emma was even more aware of the implications than I was.

"We can't do anything more about it tonight," I said. "We'll just have to keep a close watch on Linus when he comes back, and see if one of us can search his office and find it."

"Right," said Emma. "I shall have to go into his office several more times, so I may have another chance. But I absolutely must see that disc again. Without it, I have no idea what is going on."

Emma said she was feeling better and thought it was time to return home. I put on some top clothes and went to the security guard on the gate, pretending I had heard a suspicious noise at the other end of our site, and while he went to investigate, Emma slipped out.

I heard her car start, waited for the security man to report all was clear, and returned to my room. It was twenty past two.

Chapter 2

I went into work early the next morning.

I slept very little because I had spent a lot of time thinking about the extraordinary events that had just occurred.

First, what about Emma? Was she for real? Her actions, which had seemed so reasonable when she explained them, appeared rather far-fetched on further consideration. She was a nice-enough looking girl, I had to admit, but I knew nothing about her. She came in from the outside, and for all I knew she might be the front for a money-laundering racket herself. She had been remarkably frank with me – or had appeared to be. But we hadn't found this mysterious disc, even if we had, I only had her word that it belonged to Linus. What about the rest of her tale? Walking about in the middle of the night in ski-wear burgling bedrooms? A missing disc showing a fifteen million turnover? Skill in unarmed combat? She had a plausible explanation but did it really add up? I had yet to be convinced.

Why on earth should Linus be up to anything improper? He was a highly respected and professional member of the company, the very soul of uprightness and probity with an unblemished record – a model of conformity. It was in his nature. Yet he must have been up to something seriously criminal if the false accounts were as Emma had said, as there was no way in which it could be a mistake. He never made even tiny mistakes, let alone huge ones like that.

On the other hand, why should Emma come up with a story like that unless it was true? She was, after all, the employee of a very respectable firm of accountants, and was hardly likely to be involved in any dodgy enterprise involving our company. There was also no way in which she would want to lend her firm's name to any criminal financial activity. Mobilicity was a small and reasonably successful private engineering concern making wheelchairs and walking aids, but we certainly were not in the big league and therefore unlikely to be the target for any rival sabotage or financial criminality. Not on that scale, none of it made any sense.

I would have liked to believe Emma. She seemed entirely above board as we talked, and I had to admit that I felt strangely protective when I saw her all trussed up and helpless in my sellotape bonds even though I thought she was a villain at the time. She seemed a really nice person, but for all I knew she might be a brilliant actress with some other agenda, and was just having me on. I don't like being suckered.

There had to be something suspicious either about her or about Linus, and I had to admit that my instincts were with Linus at that moment.

I decided that I would have to keep an eye on both of them, but I just wished I knew what I was looking for.

Most of the morning was taken up with discussing the plans for a new walking frame which we were hoping to market. It was this I had been working late on the previous evening.

This was the brain-child of the boss, James Carwadine, who was an inspiring and innovative designer. This is what he excelled in.

Most people look at a walking frame or a wheelchair and take it for granted. It seems to take very little imagination to weld a few bars together or stick wheels on a chair, but as anyone who has had to deal with these items will know, there is a great deal more to it than that.

James had become committed to producing top-line products after first his aunt, and then his mother had needed to use frames when they became arthritic and doddery. He had pointed out to me at an early stage that a zimmer could have different functions – indoor, outdoor, for use when shopping and so on. Wheels make forward progress easier – but can be dangerous if there is no braking system. Braking systems need to be simple but effective, but also have to be operated quickly by old, slow and arthritic hands. Frames take up a great deal of room, and an ability to fold them up is a great benefit in a small bed-sit or when travelling by car – but hinged joints tend to weaken the structure and lose the rigidity which the frail walker relies on. Then there is the question of weight. Old or frail people cannot manage frames that are too heavy, and yet anyone hoping to use one say, to go shopping, would know that, while both hands are occupied, it is necessary to have some means of attaching a bag or tray to carry any purchases home. It is also desirable to have some provision for height adjustment, because each person finds their own particular preferred height – and even this may vary over time. Therefore it is a constant struggle for the manufacturer to balance all these conflicting requirements of height, weight, rigidity and other design features to produce a frame which will last and properly serve its purpose at a reasonable price.

The requirements for wheelchairs are more demanding. The problems for manufacturing electric wheel chairs are proportionately even more complicated when the size of motor and battery, and how it is recharged, and particularly the matter of weight, all have to be taken into account.

James loved the challenge of trying to juggle all these variables, and he did so with a deep knowledge of just how important his products were to frail and elderly people. He was noted for his brilliant designs because he cared about what he did, and his company worked as well as it did because he was able to share that attitude with everyone else.

Organisation and production control were not his strong points, and for some years the company had cheerily ploughed on making brilliant products using methods of Byzantine inefficiency.

This is where I came in. As a student of production engineering I had been placed in Mobilicity for work experience while I was still at College, and at once I had seen the value of the designs as well as the potential for producing them far more efficiently. James understood my enthusiasm, and appointed me as production engineer at a very decent salary as soon as I graduated from Brunel eighteen months ago. I felt I had really fallen on my feet.

I discussed the new design with James, and went through with him the plans I had been working on the day before – schedules for the production of the trade samples, tooling requirements, materials, and man-hours required for each unit when we went into full production. I knew he was particular about these details, and always insisted that the best quality materials were used, especially for moving or load-bearing parts.

"We don't want granny collapsing in a heap of tangled metal" he kept on insisting, and I respected him for it. It was another reason why his products were so highly regarded.

He finally approved the scheme I had presented, and then reminded me of the meeting he had called for all staff at one o'clock.

"I particularly want you there," he said as I left, wondering what all the urgency was about.

I took the blueprint for the new design to discuss with Gary Whitman, the senior technician.

He was the only person at Mobilicity with whom I had problems. I suspected that he had wanted the job which I had got, and it rankled him that a twenty-three year old 'college boy' was his senior. He was in his mid-thirties, and had progressed through the company from an apprenticeship scheme, so he had a natural distrust of younger people with more formal qualifications. His rich Gloucestershire burr was occasionally punctuated with some bizarre vocabulary of his own; but, because he was a good technician, most people overlooked this foible, though some other less charitable spirits mocked him behind his back. That was just too bad. I had no wish to rub him up the wrong way, but the cutting edge in his voice when he spoke to me always betrayed his resentment.

"Morning, Gary, I've just brought over James's new design to discuss with you."

He sniffed.

"I s'pose you've come to tell me 'ow to do my job, 'ave you?"

I ignored his implication.

"You'll like this. It is light, easily folded to fit into a car, but absolutely rigid when opened out. Front wheel steerable, multi-functional braking system, and the height is adjustable. It should be really stable, has a flexible pouch to carry shopping, and can be used by anyone. I think James has come up with a definite winner here, especially if we can produce it at a reasonable price."

"We always used to," he said ungraciously, implying that my input was entirely redundant. I declined to point out that they had also scarcely made a profit.

Still, he looked at the drawings, and his technician's instinct told him that it was an excellent design.

"The wheel bearings and axles will need some lathe work, but otherwise only saw, press and drill will be needed, plus the usual riveting. I've ordered the tubing of the right quality, and the hinges, which must be of stainless steel. If you can knock up half a dozen prototypes, we will test market them. End of the month?"

"I could do it by the end of next week – if I 'ad the materials." Any unavailability was obviously my fault.

"Everything was ordered yesterday. The stuff won't come today, but should be here Monday before noon. Any problems?"

"None that I'd find unaccountable," he said incongruously.

I left him to it. He was a miserable sod, but I knew that he would do a sound job even though he did seem to hate my guts.

I went for a mid-morning coffee, and noticed that Linus had returned. His neck was still considerably swollen and he appeared flushed and ill at ease.

"Glad to see you're back," I said affably.

"Er, yes," he said, somewhat distractedly. "Nasty turn. You don't expect to see wasps out so early. I have always been allergic, unfortunately."

"At least you're on the mend now."

"Yes." He paused for a moment. "However, since it's Friday, I may ask James if I can go early today. Recover fully over the weekend."

He fidgeted uncomfortably and then suddenly got up to leave.

"Must get back to my office," he muttered, and went. It might have been the effects of the sting, but he was undeniably on edge.

Emma came into the rest room.

She gave me a slight smile, and sat at another table. I had no wish to associate with her until I was sure whose side she was on.

Still, it gave me a chance to study her properly for the first time.

She looked tired, which was not surprising. The tumbling blonde locks of last night had been tied up and back and she looked every inch the professional – just as I would expect an accountant to look. She was dressed in a light blue suit with a blue and white floral design blouse reflecting the colour of her eyes, which I now noticed for the first time. However, she could not fully disguise a bruise above her left ear and though most people would not notice this, it left me with a slight feeling of guilt.

She was joined by James, and snatches of their conversation informed me that the audit would only take a few days more – probably till next Wednesday – and that she was invited to the staff meeting at one o'clock.

I returned to my office with mixed feelings. It seemed that there was only a very limited time to get to the bottom of the mystery that Emma claimed to have unearthed. The whole thing was puzzling. Emma appeared to be the classical upright accountant, concerned about an apparent irregularity. Assuming she was right, something very wrong was going on, but what? Mobilicity's books were all in perfect order, so why should anyone wish to fabricate a wholly outrageous false set? What possible purpose could it serve?

More puzzling still, who was doing it? Obviously, Linus was involved, but I found it hard to associate him with criminal activities. Was he under some sort of pressure and who would want to pressurise him – and to what purpose? There were no answers to any of these disturbing questions. After some time musing, several things became clear.

First, I couldn't escape the feeling that we had to get to the bottom of it before Emma finished the audit in the middle of next week or it would be too late. If there was no evidence of malpractice she would have to sign off the books as they were.

Secondly, we needed to get hold of that disc, assuming it existed. This was the key; it was the only evidence of any malpractice, and would also prove Emma's story; or not, as the case may be.

Thirdly, I needed to search for the disc without alerting Linus. I didn't know what his part in all this was, but certainly did not wish him to believe that I was unjustly suspicious of him.

Fourthly, I needed a strategy to achieve all these objectives.

Fifthly, I had no idea what to do next.

I toyed somewhat abstractedly with some new schedules I was working on and kept an eye on what was happening round about. Linus was shut up in his office so there was no chance of entering unobserved.

James was wandering about in an unusually purposeful manner, and I noticed that he took Emma with him on several occasions, once for a short car journey. For one awful moment I considered the possibility that he and Emma and Linus were all involved in some high financial irregularity, but a short reflection convinced me that such a thing would be impossible. That's the trouble with suspicion: if you're not careful you end up suspecting everyone.

I decided that they must be stock-taking, though why they needed to leave the site was unclear. I thought he should have been preparing for his famous staff meeting, which was fast approaching.

Gary Whitman crossed the yard, and he seemed to me to be rather more cheerful than normal, almost smug. Perhaps he thought he had come off best in his encounter with me earlier and was enjoying his imagined success, but it was hard to tell.

Otherwise, everything was as normal. Vans came and went, wheelchairs and frames were bubble-wrapped and boxed up for delivery, and the busy noises of drilling and riveting to the strains of Radio One drifted into my consciousness. People whistled as they moved things on trolleys to the next process. Fork-lifts clattered in and out of the sheds loading and unloading pallets, and from the machine shop the familiar smell of oil and flux and acetylene drifted across the main yard. This was the company at work. This is what I understood. I didn't think I was cut out for discovering financial irregularities, though I knew that I wouldn't rest easy until I knew what was happening.

I wondered if Emma had any success in locating the elusive disc, and hoped that she would at least tell me if she found it. I thought she would.

I wondered if Linus would go early and leave the disc in his office. I thought he wouldn't.

I wondered if James had any idea of anything illegal happening in his company. I was absolutely sure he hadn't.

I wondered why such a small, successful, above-board company like ours should be targeted for some improper purpose. I felt it couldn't be.

But fifteen million pounds? That clearly wasn't right, I told myself as I made for the staff meeting.

Chapter 3

James Carwadine strode purposefully into the staff meeting, and surveyed the assembled workers who were wondering what this was all about.

"Thank you all for coming," he said genially, "I won't keep you long."

He was at his best on these occasions. In his fifties, slightly boffinish, hair silvering at the temples, he had an avuncular presence which always seemed to breed confidence. This was his company; he had built it from scratch and had appointed every member himself. He had every right to feel avuncular, especially in the light of what he was about to say.

"I believe we are a first rate company," he continued. "We make a good, honest range of products which are of real use to people who would be much worse off without them. What we do is a great deal more worthwhile than making plastic models of Nelson's Column."

This raised a laugh, as he knew it would. Another firm on our small estate was well known for producing rather garish mementos for the tourist trade.

"This is, of course, the time of year when our accounts are audited, which is why Miss Crawford has been here for the last few days."

Emma gave a nod of acknowledgement, and coloured slightly.

"I am very glad to say that we have done extremely well this year. The efforts that we have always put in are really beginning to pay off. In order to recognise this achievement, I have authorised a two thousand pound bonus to be paid into your salary cheques this month."

After a moment of incredulous silence, someone broke into applause which was instantly taken up enthusiastically by everyone in the room.

He waited for the rumpus to die down, and continued, "This is to recognise the effort that the whole team have put in over the year. However, the person that we particularly have to thank for the scale of our success is our production manager, Oliver."

I had no idea he was going to do this. Every eye turned to me, and, unprepared, I didn't know where to look.

"For the last few years," he continued relentlessly, "We have got by reasonably enough, but I was aware that we ought to have been getting a greater reward for our efforts. That is why I appointed Oliver, and I have no doubt it was the right decision.

"Let me give you just two examples of what he has done. Take the special fabric for our wheelchairs. It is a very expensive raw material because it has to be strong, waterproof, fray-resistant, and breathable. The seat, back and arms are made of it, as we all know. We used to cut out all the seats from one roll, all the backs from another, and all the arms from another. One of the first things Oliver did was to rearrange the cutting so that the arms and backs were fashioned from what had previously been the waste from the seats. The result of this simple change is that we are making the same product, but saving forty seven thousand pounds on the raw materials. Most of that is now profit, which is why you have got your bonus."

He paused and looked affectionately at his company. He certainly had their attention.

"The second example is not so simple, but, believe me, it is equally important. Most of you will have experienced the new system in the Stores. You actually have to sign materials out when you need them, and you may possibly have moaned about it and felt this was a bit of bloody bureaucratic nonsense. Well, I can assure you it is not. We can now tell exactly how much we have got of whatever it is we need, and can relate that to our order book. Whereas we used to order in bulk, and have the stuff hanging around for ages, we now don't need to keep huge amounts of expensive stock lying uselessly around. I'll give you the figures. Last year we had over two hundred thousand pounds worth of goods lying around in the stockroom doing nothing for long periods. This year, it is less than fifty thousand pounds worth at any stage, and that is in there only for the minimum time necessary to make pre-ordered goods. The fact that this capital is not tied up all the time means it can be used for other purposes."

"Both of these are simple things to do, but we did not have the wit to do them until Oliver here pointed them out and saw the changes through. I think we all owe him a heartfelt round of applause."

My feelings were mixed. I was pleased to have my efforts acknowledged, but thought that such praise lavished on me, the newest recruit to the firm, seemed premature. I tried to look modest to cover my embarrassment.

"Anyway," James continued, "The result is that we not only have more income, but more capital to play with. I am therefore pleased to announce that I have bought the vacant factory site two blocks down, and we shall expand into that from next September."

He concluded with renewed thanks, and painted a bright picture for the future of the company. The meeting broke up amid a buzz of animated optimism.

During his remarks, I tried to keep my eyes to myself, but had none the less noted various points of interest.

Linus was not there.

Gary Whitman was more of a puzzle. I instinctively felt that he of all people would have reacted badly to the praise being heaped so lavishly upon me, but he seemed genuinely to join in the round of applause. Perhaps he felt he had to go with the crowd. I didn't choose to catch his eye.

Emma sat there looking cool and rather smug. She had no doubt been discussing these matters with James, and knew what was coming. She looked at me and smiled, and I realised that she, better than any one, would have realised the full force of the difference I had made to the success of the firm. That was the most warming moment of the whole embarrassing meeting; I knew I had done my bit, but the actual figures came to me as a pleasant surprise – and I was glad she would see the full significance of them.

As we moved towards lunch I accompanied her to the canteen. I didn't see any reason why I shouldn't.

"Quite the hero of the moment," she said.

"I suppose you have been plotting this with James," I said. "I wish he hadn't. I hardly knew where to look."

"Don't be so modest," she retorted. "This was a good company making a very moderate return. It is now a good company making an excellent return, and this change is down almost entirely to you. James told me he thought you were the best appointment he ever made. The figures support this theory."

I didn't know what to say to that, and decided to change the subject.

"Linus? I noticed he was not in the meeting."

She considered for a moment.

"No. I noticed that, too. I believe he left early. I went to his office several times this morning, and could see no change to the discs we looked at last night. He seemed rather distracted and it was difficult to get a sensible answer out of him. I went back later, but he had gone and the whole place was locked up."

"I suppose if the disc was that important he would have taken it with him," I said. "When everyone's gone after work I'll have a thorough search, just to make sure. If I find anything, shall I let you know?"

She agreed, and gave me her home phone number. At least that was something positive.

Over lunch, she explained that she had gone with James to look at the new premises he had acquired. Apparently he had only just signed the papers to clinch the deal, and wanted to show them off. She thought they would be far preferable to our present site, and would allow for the possibility of steady expansion. I appreciated her encouraging report, and the fact that she appeared to have an interest in Mobilicity's success.

Friday afternoon is never a time when much happens, but on this particular Friday there seemed to be an unusual spring in the step of our employees. They could look forward not only to the weekend, but to a secure future for the firm, to being appreciated and, of course, to two grand.

I had completed all the immediate work in hand, having agreed the new project with James and sorted out the details with Gary, so I relaxed in my office and did a bit of thinking.

My first thought was that I had enjoyed having lunch with Emma. Well, who wouldn't? She was an attractive girl, and she seemed genuinely interested in the company, and made some ego-boosting remarks about my part in it. Very gratifying, especially as she, having worked on the books, would be uniquely aware of how much influence I might have had.

Then another thought struck me, and it came as something of a shock. Perhaps she was being too interested in the working of the firm - and too ready to flatter my ego. What if she was sussing us out for some unknown opposition?

I tried to think this through. We were an attractive company, just breaking into a really profitable future. James had some excellent designs which might be of interest to anyone trying to buy us out and reap the benefit from our expertise – after all, for some years we had been under-exploiting our products, and someone else may have realised this. A detailed knowledge of our books and a sight of our future plans would be invaluable to them. Alternatively, a rival manufacturer might wish to promote their own designs by taking ours off the market. Suppose someone else really was after our designs? Was that what Emma had really been trying to find the previous night? I only had her word for the mysterious disc, and apart from that there was absolutely no evidence that it had ever existed. Suppose Linus was as honest as I assumed him to be, and had no suspicious disc in his office? That assumption made the whole of Emma's story a load of rubbish, and could only mean that she was playing me along for some ulterior reason.

I have never felt so out of control. Something was seriously wrong, but I could get no line on what the problem was, let alone who was on whose side. Was Emma spying on Mobilicity? Was Linus a crook? I was still in a complete fog of indecision when it was time to go home.

I rang the garage, but they told me the paint on the wing needed more time to dry, so I borrowed one of Mobilicity's little white vans to use over the weekend.

I didn't see Emma leave, but decided to return to my flat and let things calm down. Then I would return and make a thorough search for that elusive disc. If I could find any trace of that, it would settle the matter one way or the other.

I drove to the supermarket to get my weekend shopping, and it must have been about twenty past six when I parked the van and carried the goods up the steps to my front door. I unlocked it, and was just stooping down to pick up the bags when I felt my arms being pinioned from behind, my jacket collar being pulled back down to my elbows, and a thick sack-like bag pulled over my head and shoulders. I was twisted round several times, and lost all sense of position.

There was no way I could attempt to strike back. I had no idea who my assailants were, or how many. I felt totally at their mercy.

I was bundled into my flat and thrown down roughly into an easy chair.

A voice spoke quietly into my left ear.

"We can make this easy or hard. Where is it?"

"Where is what?"

Someone's hand smashed hard into my left cheek.

"Stop trying to be funny. You know perfectly well what we want, the disc."

"I haven't got any bloody disc. I don't even know what disc you are talking about."

Smash. The voice was less gentle, more laced with menace this time.

"Stop playing games. We know you must have it – either you or the girl. You were seen going into the office last night."

This was a serious blow. How could they have known Emma and I had searched the office? I tried to buy myself some time to think by stalling.

"Well, of course Miss Crawford and I went to the office last night. She had lost some important papers, and asked me to help her to look for them. I don't know anything about a disc. What was on it?"

He hesitated uncertainly for just a moment. Smash again.

"I don't believe you. People don't go wandering about after midnight searching through offices unless they have a purpose. Lost papers could wait till the morning. This disc was more important than that, and it was there earlier; it was not there after you two had gone ferreting about. So, where is it?"

"Look," I said quickly before he could strike again, "It's no good you going on hitting me, I don't know what disc you are talking about. I have never seen it, and I certainly haven't got it. There is nothing more I can say."

He hit me again, this time on the right cheek.

"How am I supposed to get through to you?" I shouted desperately. My whole head was ringing with the blows, and I had no way of guessing from which direction the next one would come. I needed time to think. "I just don't know what you're on about. What's supposed to be on this disc, anyway?"

"That's for me to know, and you to wonder about. You can hold out for as long or short a time as you like, but I intend to have that disc so you might just as well make it easier on yourself."

Smash on the left cheek again. At that moment his mobile rang.

"OK, you've got her then? Right, any sign of the disc? No? Not in her room. Where have you taken her? Oh yes, that'll be fine - well off the beaten track, and deserted. No chance of being looked for there. You stay on guard, no hard stuff until I tell you, as we arranged. Make no calls, and take no calls except from me. Only release her when I tell you, and not until."

He rang off.

"I expect you heard all that, and can guess what it was about. Yes, we have Miss Crawford. She does not have the disc either, or so she says."

His voice became menacingly insistent.

"I want that disc; it is mine, and I intend to get it back. You and Miss Crawford were seen going into the Accounts office in the middle of last night, after which the disc went missing. It was certainly there earlier.

"Therefore, either you or Miss Crawford must have it. We shall keep her as a security for the safe return of my property. You will receive telephoned instructions about how to return it tomorrow at lunchtime, here at your flat. You will be given a deadline by which to produce it."

"Failure to produce the disc as required will have the unpleasant result of you being sent the top joint of one of Miss Crawford's fingers for each period of four hours you fail to give me what I want." He paused, letting the awful implication of his threat sink in.

"I believe you do have the disc, and suggest that it will save a lot of unpleasantness if you deliver it as I tell you. In the unlikely event of you not knowing where the disc is, then I suggest you make a maximum effort to find it.

"I hope I make myself clear."

His hand smashed into my right cheek once more for luck.

"By the way," he said, "I noticed that you didn't lock your van. You should. There are some real rogues about. I'll be in touch."

I heard him departing, pulling the door shut quietly behind him, and I was left alone with a headache.

Chapter 4

It took me several minutes to free myself from my restrictions. I had to rub the hood up and down the back of the chair, gradually easing it off until I could shake the thing free. At least, I could see again. Until then, I never realised how constricting a jacket could be when pulled backwards down to the elbows, and it took me several efforts to work it over my shoulders into its proper place. I was now in a position to resume normal life again, and take stock.

I went into the bathroom to inspect the damage inflicted by his blows. Fortunately, the thickness of the material had prevented the skin from being broken, and apart from some puffiness and possible bruising on the left side there was nothing that would not clear up in a day or so. This was a relief. When I was blindfold my imagination tended to exaggerate the extent of the blows.

I poured myself a beer and sat down to do some serious thinking. My immediate reaction was one of anger. How dare anyone come and attack me in my own home, render me helpless, bash me about, and make wholly unreasonable demands which I could not meet? I had never felt as vulnerable as in those few minutes under that hood. There was no way of telling which side the next blow would fall, or when, and I was unable to brace myself to take it. I had no idea who my assailants were, or how I could do anything except what they told me. I was entirely at their mercy, and I hated them for it.

I was also appalled by their leader's demands. It certainly appeared that there was a disc, and it obviously had a huge importance for someone. At least that part of Emma's story was confirmed. If she really was an innocent party, and had been taken as some sort of hostage for the return of the disc, I felt physically sick at the thought of the threats that had been made about removing the tops of her fingers.

But then, suppose I was intended to feel like that? If there was a disc, and some outside party wanted it, and Emma was working for them but couldn't get hold of it, then they could easily have manufactured the phone call I had just heard in order to pressurise me.

The more I thought about it, the more I felt that there must be a missing disc, and somehow everything depended upon its retrieval.

Yet there was nothing I could do about it. I had no idea where the bloody disc was, or how I could meet his demands. My assailant clearly refused to believe I hadn't got it. But I didn't have it, and Emma didn't have it. How the hell was I supposed to produce it?

These emotions of anger and angst occupied me for several minutes, until I remembered the old saying, 'Don't get angry, get even'. That was fine – but how was I to get even? It was time for some analysis.

First, who was this assailant I was facing? I knew I couldn't give him what he wanted, but tried to form a picture of the kind of person I was up against. It clearly wasn't Linus; I'd have recognised his dry voice anywhere.

I'd not managed to get a sight of him, so I had to rely on some fleeting impressions gained during the course of his presence. I caught a glimpse of his feet, and noticed that he wore expensive shoes. They were the sort that you see in exclusive shops labelled 'Italian' and 'Hand-sewn' and cost two hundred pounds. He was obviously not a crude thug.

This impression was borne out by the vocabulary he used. He sounded like a solicitor, or an old-fashioned schoolmaster. There were the give-away words and phrases like, 'that's for me to know, and you to wonder about', and 'I intend to have that disc,' and 'we shall keep her as a security for the safe return of my property'. This was classic middle class, even public school, professional talk spoken in a stockbroker-belt accent.

I found this depressing. My assailant seemed to be an intelligent and probably well-connected opponent. He was unlikely to be a push-over.

Next, I wondered where he got his information from. I was severely shaken by his assertion that Emma and I had been seen going into Linus' office the night before. There was nobody about, apart from the security guard on the gate, and he was way outside while we were in the building. How could my attacker have known, and known so quickly? To the best of my knowledge, nobody had realised the disc was missing at the time, so why should anyone be keeping watch? I could find no answer to this. Then I considered the disc.

Neither I nor Emma knew exactly what the false accounts meant, but it was quite obviously of great importance to somebody. Its significance was clear from the speed and violence of the attempts to get it back.

This raised the real heart of the problem – where was the disc now? If Linus didn't have it, and they didn't have it, and neither Emma nor I had it, where the hell was it? How was I going to be able to retrieve it before Emma started to lose her fingers?

I could think of nothing but Plan A, which was for me to go and have a thorough search of Linus' office. I did not hold out much hope of finding it there, but I supposed there might be some slim chance that it had somehow been overlooked. I heaved myself up and returned to Mobilicity.

It was early evening now, and the security guard let me in, enquiring genially if I had also been stung on the face. I made some non-committal reply, and made for Linus' office. I unlocked the door with my master key.

The room was just as I had last seen it. I made a thorough search of the obvious places, and then opened all the drawers and checked underneath and behind them. I looked behind pictures, under the rug, down the back of the chair and even under his pot plant. There was absolutely nothing that could hide the missing disc. I checked inside all the disc cases to see if there were any discrepancies between the names on the case and on the disc, but there were none. I checked them on the computer to see if they could have been deliberately been changed over, but none had. Everything was as it should be.

Depressed, I left the office, locking the door before walking back down the corridor to the main entrance.

I wondered who could have seen us entering the office last night, and looked casually round as I sauntered slowly back.

Then I got it. CCTV.

It is one of those things that happen when you are used to working in a building every day you tend to forget the familiar fixtures and fittings. We had always had a simple closed circuit television system on the site, and this must have been how we had been spotted.

I raced back to the security office on the gate, and asked the guard if I could run back some of yesterday's tape.

"No problem," he said. "When do you want to go from?"

"I'd like to run slowly back from about one o'clock this morning."

"Okay." He fast-reversed until he reached the necessary place.

"If you're going to be here for a bit, I'll leave you with it and do the rounds, if that's all right with you."

"Fine. I'll stay here till you get back."

He left, and I concentrated on the monitor. After a period of nothing, there we were, Emma and I retreating out of the office. Then nothing again. Finally, there we were, entering the corridor.

I ran it back to the moment when we first appeared, changed to forward and viewed our entrance and exit in normal time.

I had to admit that, seen on the video, we made a highly suspicious pair. I was in my jeans; she was in a ski-suit, as we crept furtively in and out of the office. It was not in the least surprising that anyone, seeing that, would assume we were up to no good.

Without thinking, I switched the tape back to reverse.

The security guard returned shortly after.

"Everything okay?" he enquired.

"Yes, fine," I replied randomly, thinking of other things.

"It's funny," he said, "You're the second person today who has wanted to see that tape."

"Really?" I suddenly started to take notice. "Who else?"

"Linus McEwan. He asked to see it at lunchtime. He seemed a bit strange then, and was even more so when he came in later asking for the key to the new factory we're having."

I didn't pay much attention to his last comment since I was delighted to have one puzzle solved.

So, that's who had seen us. It was blindingly obvious that Linus, if he had seen what I had just seen, would have inevitably have assumed we had got his precious disc. But it still didn't explain who it was who attacked me.

I stood there, uncertain what to do next, staring idly at the monitor. I saw Emma leave after entering at twenty to six.

There was the same empty corridor - but suddenly I noticed another person exiting and then entering the accounts office .

I stopped the tape, and set it to replay forward in real time.

There it was, timed at twenty past five yesterday afternoon. A figure, looking round furtively, slowly entered the office, and a moment or two later re-emerged, fitting something small into his jacket pocket. He had no business to be anywhere near that office. He looked anxiously round, then left by the main entrance.

So that's who had got the disc. Gary Whitman.

I went to my own office for a few moments to digest this information.

I reckoned it had to be Gary who had stolen the disc, and would at least know where it was. Unfortunately, he was the last person I wanted to deal with. I had no idea what his part in all this was, but guessed that he would do almost anything to spite me if it came to co-operation.

I went into the admin office and looked up Gary's address. He lived in a flat on Rodborough Hill, not far away. I drove back to my own flat to work out a plan of campaign. The more I thought about it, the more I was sure he had the disc. The question was - how could I get him to give it up? If he was working for the other side, whoever they were, he was unlikely to be of any assistance. But then, if he was one of them, they would know where the disc was, and not be hassling me for it.

My real problem was that I had no idea of what was going on, who was on whose side, and what the hell this was all about. All I knew for certain was that I had to get the disc or risk Emma being mutilated. I really couldn't face that.

I came to the conclusion that I would have to confront Gary, and gamble on the possibility that he was not one of them, whoever they were. And on the assumption that he had no motives similar to theirs. And on the hope that I could persuade him to work with me.

I grabbed a cheese sandwich, and got into the van to drive to confront Gary. I was only too aware that I did not know what I was doing, or how I was going to approach Gary, or what my reception would be. I only knew I had to do something.

It was twenty to nine when I arrived at his flat.

Chapter 5

I rang the bell and had to wait some time until he responded.

"Hello, Gary," I said in a neutral voice.

"Oh. It's you. I s'pose you'd better come in."

I had expected a more hostile reception, and went in feeling a bit more hopeful.

Gary's flat was more or less as I expected. Not very large, not very tidy, but perfectly reasonable for a thirty-three year old bachelor living by himself. Off-duty, he looked exactly as he did at work, slim, scruffy, with sandy hair, blue eyes and grubby finger nails. He appeared to have settled himself down to watch telly with a six-pack and a pizza.

There was an awkward silence which he was the first to break.

"There's something I want to say," he muttered, and then paused.

"I'm listening," I said, hoping to break the ice and get his measure before coming to the point.

"I'm sorry I've been giving you a bad time," he burst out suddenly. "I'd been counting on getting your job."

There was not a lot I could say to this, except a neutral "Oh."

"It was only today that I realised that I couldn't do what you've done, when the boss started explaining about the profit."

"Well, it's what I've been trained to do," I pointed out quietly.

"That's it," he said, warming to the subject. "Those things were right under my nose, and 'ave been for the last ten years. I never saw 'em, but you picked 'em up in a few weeks. That's the difference. I'd never 'ave done it."

"Don't talk yourself down," I told him. "You are a bloody good technician, and James needs you just as much as he needs me. It's just that we have different roles to play."

"Yeah," he replied, "But you make the money."

"And you make the wheelchairs. Without them there would be nothing to sell. We need each other."

I looked straight at him.

"While we are about it, let's get this 'college boy' thing straight. Yes, I went to college, but that's because you have to these days. I was the first one of my family to go. I learned some useful things there, some technical, like use of materials, some practical, like drawing up different sorts of contracts. But most of what I know about stock control I learnt from my father, who ran an ironmongery shop – you know, the sort of place which sells everything from firebricks to carpet tacks. He wouldn't have lasted three months if he held stock like Mobility used to. It's common sense, really."

I could see him reassessing his image of me.

"Shake on it?" I suggested.

He got up and shook my hand so warmly that I felt I was almost in a position to move on to the next stage of my mission. But before I could do so he offered me a can of Boddingtons and said, "If I didn't get the extra salary, at least I got the extra two grand. I needed that."

"Problems?" I enquired.

He looked at me speculatively. After a few moments of uncertainty, he decided that he could trust his new-found friend, and it all came out.

He told me that his parents had both been killed in a car crash nine years ago, and he had felt responsible for his younger brother Steve, who was several years his junior and had done well at school.

"Better than me," he said matter-of-factly. "'e got good A-levels and went to college to study computer sciences. That's when the trouble started."

"Trouble?"

"Yeah. 'e insociated with a lot of wasters – public school types, as far as I could tell, and they all 'ad too much money and no sense. 'e seemed to think they were cool. Worst thing 'e ever did. That's why I don't 'ave much time for college boys."

"Most students aren't like that," I pointed out.

"I s'pose not. But those are the only ones I've 'ad contact with. Anyway, the up and down of it is that they did drugs. 'e couldn't 'andle it, and before 'e knew what 'ad 'appened 'e was 'ooked. It took less than a couple of weeks, 'e told me." There was a despondent pause.

"Crack. 'e smoked it. It acts faster, gives you a bigger buzz, but doesn't last 'ardly five minutes. Once you start you need more and more larger doses more and more often. It was cheap and a bit of 'armless fun to start off, but 'e ended up being addictivated."

There was a long pause. I felt genuinely sorry for him, but there was very little I could say that would be much comfort. I could only help him share his problem.

"What happened?" I asked as gently as I could.

"What do you think? 'e dropped out of college, and drifted around on benefits as best 'e could. 'e went on needing crack, and always more of it. It's unmerciless once it gets 'old, and 'e ended up with a 'abit which 'e said cost several 'undred pounds a week, though I think it might have been a lot more. I knew 'e was in trouble, but 'e refused to talk to me about it for a long time.

"A couple of months ago, 'e came to me to tell me 'e realised 'e 'ad to do something, and 'e finally admitted that 'e had become a dealer to afford enough of the stuff for 'imself. 'e was supplied with a large quantity, took what 'e needed, and pushed to rest. The profits 'e 'ad to pay back, or 'e wouldn't be supplied with no more."

"So he was simply taking all the risk in selling the stuff in return for what he needed? Bloody hell, there's no future in that."

"Course there ain't. 'e came to me to tell me 'e realised that, but 'e didn't know what to do about it. 'e could see no way out. 'e needed the crack, 'e couldn't just give it up. So, 'e 'ad to go somewhere to get 'elp. 'e thought that if he went to the proper authorities, it was sure to come out that 'e was a dealer, and that would mean a gaol sentence. 'e could go to one of those private detox places, but that would be expensive, and 'e didn't have that kind of money. 'e asked me to 'elp. If nothing was done, 'e would end up either dead or in prison for a very long time." There was another pause. I didn't interrupt.

"That's why I needed the money. 'e's my kid brother. What would you 'ave done?"

"God knows," I said. "I don't envy you."

"I made some enquiries about private clinics, but no way could I afford them. They seem to specialise in the addictations of the rich."

His misery was as obvious as his dilemma.

He looked at me earnestly, wondering if he should take me completely into his confidence. He decided he might as well.

"Can I trust you?" he asked simply.

"I'll do anything I can to help," I said, and meant it.

"Well, Steve knows the fix 'e's in, and 'e also knows that if 'e is to 'ave any life at all 'e's gotta get out. The drugs world has no pity and little chance of escape unless you 'ave more money than ordinary people like us 'ave got. 'e says if 'e can't get off drugs, 'e'll overdose, and that'll be an end to it."

Again a pause.

"'owever, 'e got hold of a piece of information that could 'elp. There is one major dealer in this area, the local Mr Big, 'oo is the main supplier to suckers like Steve. 'e 'as an army of Steves working for 'im on the same 'opeless terms. I think 'e controls most of the area between Bristol and Cheltenham. Well, Steve found out by chance that Mr Big – I don't know 'is name – 'as to launder all 'is drug money to avoid being traced by the Revenue or the Drugs Squad. 'e does this by processing it through a legitimate account. You'll never guess in a million years which account 'e uses."

I was already ahead of him, but let him continue.

"Mobilicity."

I raised my eyebrows.

"Yes," he continued. "Bloody Mr Honesty Linus McEwan, our revered accountant."

I pretended to be astonished into silence.

"Steve told me that 'e'd somehow found out that this drugs racket was probably being laundered through a false account at our office, and that everything was on one special disc. We decided that if we could get 'old of that disc, we could sell it back to them for enough money to detox Steve. I didn't know whether to believe 'im, but 'e seemed convinced so it was worth a shot. Well, yesterday, after work, I went into Linus' office when 'e'd gone off to 'ospital and there was nobody about. I looked for the disc. I didn't really know what I was looking for, but one seemed different from the rest, and was labelled 'Mobilicity 2' - so I took it."

He nodded at his desk.

"It's over there."

A feeling of intense relief engulfed me. Several things immediately became clear. I now knew that there was a disc, why it was important – and, unbelievably, where it was. I also knew that Emma was absolutely on the level, and her story had been true all along. I could see why she was worried, and so anxious to clear up the mystery disc. I felt almost ashamed and ungracious for ever having doubted her, and could only imagine the distress her capture would cause her. There was no way she could guess I would find the disc.

In the same instant I realised they were holding her hostage, I had no doubt that they would carry out their grisly threat. I could hardly bear to think about it.

Gary continued, "I don't know 'ow much use it will be. I've tried it on my computer, and I can't read it. I can't even copy it - it's got some sort of control. I'm going to see Steve on Sunday, and we'll try to work out 'ow to negotiate with them. It is going to be difficult. People like them don't like being messed around, and can turn nasty."

I could confirm this last judgement.

It was clear that Gary had now confided everything to me, and trusted me. He was probably glad to unburden himself of the problem which had clearly been worrying him silly. Well, if he could trust me, I reckoned I should trust him.

"Gary", I said quietly, "I knew you had the disc. That's why I'm here."

A look of horror crossed his face.

"Bloody 'ell, you're not one of them, are you?"

"No way. Certainly not. Just listen for a moment. I knew you had it because I saw you on the CCTV. You see, Miss Crawford found out about the dodgy disc by accident while she was doing the audit, and she and I went to try and get hold of it after you had taken it. When they realised it was missing, they thought to play back the CCTV tape. We were seen, presumably by Mr McEwan, on the play-back because we were the last ones into his office. It didn't occur to him that anyone might have taken it earlier."

I outlined the story of the previous night, and how suspicious we must have looked, and finally I told him of the ultimatum I had received that evening.

"So they now believe I have the disc, and if I don't return it, they are going to chop off her fingers until they get it," I concluded.

He listened with close attention

"So you knew I 'ad it all along?"

"Only for the last hour or so. But I can quite see why you wanted it."

We both sat in silence for a while, trying to take on board the complications that had been revealed.

Finally I said, "It comes down to this. You need the disc to get your brother off drugs, and I need it to stop bits of Miss Crawford's fingers from being cut off. What a choice."

He thought for a while, then said, "I suppose if they knew I 'ad the disc, they would let Miss Crawford go?"

"I doubt they'd release Miss Crawford until they actually had the disc. Why would they? Even if they did let her go, but knew you had it, they wouldn't hesitate to beat you or your brother up till you gave it to them. Or they could simply cut off his crack supply. You can't reason with them - I've told you what they did to me. Do you think they would let you just keep their precious disc until they paid up for it? No chance. They're not like that."

His face fell. He could see I was right.

"What are we going to do?" He sounded desperate.

"I don't know. Let me think."

So far, my main concern, apart from my original curiosity about its contents, had been to deliver the disc in return for Emma's safety. Now there were two other dimensions to the importance of the disc – the plight of Gary's brother, and the huge criminal scam that was having its profits laundered at Mobilicity. Simply giving the disc back to them would, at the best, address only one of these areas, and there was no guarantee of that.

There was a long pause.

"I suppose we could call the police, though we don't know where she is, so it might be a wild goose chase. In any case, I don't think they would be very likely to come out on a Friday night just on the off-chance."

Gary looked troubled. "If they did, the 'ole story is bound to come out. They'd do Steve for bein' a pusher."

I tried to think of other approaches but was about to admit defeat when Gary spoke.

"Is there any chance of us rescuing Miss Crawford? That would give us more optionals."

He was right, of course, and it would relieve me of my main concern.

"Good, let's think about it. What have we got? I heard them discussing the fact that she was somewhere out of the way."

"'ow long has she been 'eld by 'em?" he asked.

"It couldn't have been very long, because her captor had only just got her there. I should think that was about six o'clock this evening."

"Well, they couldn't 'ave 'ad much time to arrange anywhere to 'old 'er. If it was out of the way, and secure, and improbable to be noticed, it would be difficult to find a place like that." Gary could be remarkably perceptive, it seemed.

"You're right. I imagine that Mr McEwan had seen the CCTV tape at lunchtime, and told his colleagues. They must have decided to tackle me after work, and hold Miss Crawford as a hostage in case I didn't give them what they wanted. They were absolutely convinced I had their sodding disc. "That's your fault," I said in mock accusation. "If I hadn't seen you on the tape when I was in the security office…."

I broke off. There was something buzzing about in the back of my mind that I knew was important – something to do with what I had seen earlier. Something in the Security Office.

I tried to picture the scene. I had gone to look at the video tape, and seen our escapade the night before. Then the tape ran back further, which was when I noticed Gary. No, that wasn't it.

The security guard had been on his rounds; it was something he said when he came back, after he told me Linus had also looked at the tape earlier.

I suddenly recalled his words – 'Mr McEwan was even more strange when he came in later asking for the key to the new factory we're having'.

That had to be it.

"I think I know where they've got her," I said.

I told Gary what I'd heard, and he looked impressed.

"Do you think we can get 'er out?"

I was wondering the same.

"There must be a chance. They won't be expecting us to find her, and from what they said on the phone to each other there would only be one guard there. There're two of us are you up for it?"

He didn't hesitate for a moment. "When do we start?"

We decided to go in the van. He put on some trainers and a dark sweatshirt, and I drove back to my flat to change into a tracksuit. I also collected various things I could imagine we might need: a torch, some bolt cutters, a knife, some parcel tape, some rope and a tarpaulin. I thought those would be enough, together with the other odds and ends in the van.

It was only a five minute drive to the site of the empty factory which was to be our new home. The whole area was deserted, and had the dead air of dereliction that accompanies a site that is not actively in use. The only light came from the street-lamps some distance away, and from a moon that appeared fitfully from behind broken clouds. Black paint flaked off the iron railings, and I made a mental note that this would all have to have a proper scrape-down, undercoat and finish when we took over.

I parked just outside the gate, which I was surprised to find unlocked, and we cautiously approached the building itself. A nearby clock was striking ten.

Chapter 6

The factory buildings were situated on a large site, and consisted of one main shed apparently surrounded by three smaller units which were presumably there for storage and administrative purposes. They were built mostly of concrete and corrugated asbestos, typical of many of the industrial properties to be found in the valleys radiating out from Stroud. They are not pretty, and they are not modern, but at least they are functional and provide work for a surprisingly large number of people.

"Where do we start?" asked Gary.

"Well, the smaller units seem the most likely place, so I think we should look at them first and leave the main building till last. We'll start with this one, which looks as though it was the main office. We'll stick together. No noise until we have located them."

We cautiously approached the first building. There was no sign of occupation, but this could be explained by the fact that there were heavy steel shutters drawn down over the windows, which made it very difficult to decide if there was anyone inside. We tried listening at the windows, but heard nothing, so we gave up on that one.

The whole site was reasonably clear in occasional moonlight and the glow from the street lamps, and when we became fully accustomed to the light we realised that all the buildings were shut up in the same way.

"It's going to be diabolical 'ard finding anyone in this," commented Gary with some concern. "I thought we'd see where they were right away."

"Yes," I said. "But our only chance is that they are here, so we'd better make sure. Two more outbuildings to go."

We inspected both of the others units with the same result. There was no sign of life in either, but we couldn't be sure. The shutters made it impossible to see anything inside. If those shutters were there to keep burglars out, they did an excellent job. The buildings smelt of damp and neglect, and appeared deserted. It was all very depressing.

"Come on, then," I said, "We'd better have a look at the main building."

We walked round the back, on the side away from the road and there we saw it. One BMW carefully parked out of sight of the public.

"That settles it. They have to be here somewhere," I said triumphantly.

"'ave to be," he agreed.

We slowly surveyed the whole of the building. There were no windows lower down as it was built with roof-lights in the traditional way for factory buildings. We moved back to see if we could detect any suggestion of light coming from the top, but we couldn't, so we moved close to listen for any sound.

There was nothing. I was sure they were on the site somewhere but it was hard to see what more we could do to pin-point them.

We stood back from the main block and wondered what to do next.

"What's that over there?" Gary suddenly said, pointing. Right at the back of the site, furthest away from the road, we noticed in the shadows a single storey building about twenty feet square. Double doors were set beneath a large flat slab of concrete supported by metal uprights which served as a porch.

This was different from the others. There were bars on the outside, and the shutters had been fixed to the inside of the windows.

"What do you think this was?" Gary asked.

"Dunno. I suppose it must have been a special store for something dangerous, or valuable, which was needed in their manufacturing process. Cyanide or acid or gold leaf or something. It would make an excellent prison. Let's investigate."

We walked carefully round the side, and then came to the darkened rear of the shed.

"Look," whispered Gary.

The windows were shuttered like those at the front; but from the bottom of the second window three small rays of light illuminated the shadows.

"That's it. It has to be them." I felt a momentary exultation.

However, it took less than a moment more to realise that knowing where they were was one thing, but getting Emma out safely was quite another. We had no idea of who was holding her. I guessed there would only be one guard, but he could well be armed. We couldn't simply knock on the door and say, 'Excuse me, but can we have Miss Crawford back?' and hope for a result.

We retreated to the other side of the main building to work out some sort of plan.

"There's no way we can break in and surprise them," I said. "The windows are too well barred and shuttered. That's hopeless."

"Could we make a racket outside, and get 'im to come out?" suggested Gary. "Then the two of us could grab 'im."

"Um," I said dubiously. "I think a racket would put him on his guard. What would we do if he just ignored us? Or came out armed? We'll have to come up with something else."

"How about scratching the door gently?" said Gary. "That would not be threatening, and might make 'im come out to see what it was."

"You come up with some original ideas," I said, impressed. I had not thought of Gary as a lateral thinker. "The only difficulty is that we both have to be ready to grab him when he comes out, and if one of us is scratching that might be difficult. It would be ideal if we could lure him out and drop on him from the flat porch above the doorway. That would be our best way to catch him off guard."

"Okay, but how are we going to make sure 'e comes out?"

We pondered this for a while, until Gary suggested, "Why not light a fire in the doorway?"

This showed real promise. At the smell of smoke, he would be bound to investigate. On the other hand, if he saw a small bonfire in the entrance, he would know that it had been put there deliberately, and would instantly be suspicious. Still, it was a good idea, and I said so.

We went back towards the shed, hoping for inspiration. I looked round and focussed on the BMW some twenty yards away in the gloom.

An idea began to take shape.

"How about this?" I said. "We will use your idea of lighting a fire, but we'll position it by his car. At the same time we will try to make some smoke fumes waft into the shed. The idea is that he will smell smoke, come to the door to see what is happening, and see his car apparently going up in flames. What do you think he'll do?"

"''e'll run straight over to see what's 'appening anyone would."

"Exactly," I said. "And he'll be concentrating on his car, and off his guard and he won't stand dithering in the doorway. We'll tackle him as soon as he steps beyond the porch."

Enthused by the thought of the general plan, we mulled over the details.

There was no problem about starting the fire, as there was plenty of waste and rubbish lying about. I had a spare tin of oil in the van, and Gary had a cigarette lighter. We wondered whether to set the car on fire for real, but thought this might cause it to explode and cause confusion and attract unwanted attention, so we decided that a cheerful blaze just in front of the car would do just as well.

"Pity," said Gary. "I wouldn't 'ave minded setting light to the bastard's BMW."

Then there was the question of smoke for the shed. A smouldering oily rag would produce the right sort of effect, but we had to make sure the fumes were detected inside.

We went back to the shed and looked at it more closely. The metal door was a tight fit, and the windows were shuttered and useless for our purpose.

"What's those?" whispered Gary suddenly, pointing upwards.

"Of course, air vents. Let's have a closer look." I examined the two circular holes high up in the side wall.

One of them appeared to have jammed shut, but the other one had slats which yielded immediately to my touch. I had no idea what part of the shed this particular vent led from, but it would have to do. The trouble was that it would be impossible to judge how long it would need to take effect.

With the fires sorted out, we considered how best to tackle BMW Bastard when he came out.

We knew we would have the advantage of surprise, especially if we were above him on the porch while his attention was on his car. However, we had no idea what he was like, how big he was, how used to fighting, or how he might be armed. Sure, there were two of us, but we were amateurs.

"We want something like a net to drop over 'im," Gary shrewdly observed.

We didn't have a net. Still, he was quite right. Dropping something over him would be the quickest way of immobilising him. I had an idea.

"Come round to the front office with me," I said.

"Why?"

"You'll see," I said, and he followed me there.

Standing at the front entrance was a number of different coloured wheelie-bins. I pointed to them.

"How about taking one of those, and lifting it on to the porch. Then, with one of us each side, we'll drop it over his head when he comes out. It will immobilise his arms, and he won't be expecting anything like that. Do you think it would work?"

"Don't see why not. Yeah. Let's give it a go and when 'e's in it, we could turn it upside down – that would really fix 'im. I should like that."

I began to detect a vindictive streak in Gary with which I entirely sympathised.

It was in a spirit of ruthless elation that we made our final plans.

We selected a suitable bin and carried it to the front of the shed. I climbed on to the porch using the handrail at the side, and Gary handed me the bin, which I upended to await our return.

Having climbed down, I went back to the van and collected the oil tin, the parcel tape, the rope and the knife.

Gary meanwhile collected a pile of leaves, dry twigs, some damp sacking and an assortment of bits of wood which, when lit with some of my oil, would produce a good combination of smoke and flame.

He also found what appeared to be an old hand towel which would make an ideal medium for the fumes in the shed. I poured more oil into the towelling and allowed time for it to seep thoroughly into the fabric. We were almost ready.

"Right," I said. "If you can light this now, I will go and place it carefully into the vent. I expect it will take at least two or three minutes for him to pick up the smell, and wonder what to do about it. I'm banking on him guessing the smoke is coming from outside. As soon as I've done that I'll get up on the porch and wait for you there.

"You go up to his car and light the bonfire. We want it to look an authentic blaze, so make sure it is going well before you leave it and join me on the porch. I should think you will have three or four minutes' leeway. Then we just wait till he comes out. We hope."

"'e will. 'e's got to," said Gary, lighting the oily towelling in my hand.

It took a while to get going, but when I breathed on the seat of the flame a red glow appeared, immediately accompanied by pungent fumes. Gary left, and I carefully carried the smouldering material and fed it between the slats in the vent I had identified. I assured myself that the burn was going nicely, returned quickly and climbed up on to the porch with the wheelie-bin. I taped the lid back so that it wouldn't flap around when we dropped it, and waited for Gary.

I could clearly see him attempting to light the fire by the BMW. He was having some trouble getting it going, but found a bit of tin sheet with which he fanned it vigorously. It seemed to be taking him for ever, and I was concerned that he would be caught in the act. However, bright flames suddenly blazed out, accompanied by a thick billow of blackish fumes.

He stood back admiring his handiwork.

"Come on," I said under my breath. Almost as though he had heard me, he turned and trotted back to the porch.

We waited on tenterhooks, one each side of the wheelie-bin. We seemed to be waiting for ever, though it could only have been for a minute or two. From inside the shed there came the sound of movement. A door opened and closed, and there was the sound of some mild expletives. Then we heard the sound of keys in the front door, which was opened cautiously.

For a moment he stood under the porch, but almost immediately the fire blazing by the car caught his attention.

"What the ……. ?" he managed to say as he started forward.

A wheelie-bin enveloped him.

Gary and I just had time for quick high-fives before clambering to the ground. It took both of us to up-end him.

BMW Bastard was upside down and helpless inside the bin, though his legs stuck out of the top. I took my parcel tape and bound his ankles together tightly. Here we go again, I thought.

He was obviously confused, but we needed him to be far more securely bound before we could let him out.

I said to Gary, "Can you pull him gradually out of the bin by his legs?"

"Yeah. I think so. I'll loop the rope round 'is ankles, and stand on the porch to 'eave 'im up."

It worked as our victim did not seem too heavily built.

I spoke into the bin. "Listen to me. You can choose to stay upside down in this bin which we will tie into an upright position. If you reckon you could get out of it by yourself, good luck."

"Sod off." Our bin-filler didn't seem too pleased.

"Alternatively," I continued conversationally, "my friend here will slowly pull you up by the ankles, but you will place your hands behind your back, and I will tape them up before you are fully out. Any attempt to struggle or escape will mean that my friend here simply drops you back head first into the bin. Won't you Gary?"

"It'll be a real pleasure," said Gary, laughing.

I addressed the bin again.

"Which is it to be? Stay as you are, or let us secure you in a civilised way? It's up to you."

A surly voice muttered, "Bastards, get me out of here."

"You understand? Any trouble, and you go straight back in, and stay there."

There was what I took to be a grudging acceptance from within.

"Okay, my friend will start pulling you up. Put your hands behind your back, palms together, and keep them there."

He gradually emerged from the bin, too shaken to do anything except what he was told. I quickly bound his hands and wrists with the parcel tape until I was satisfied he was completely secure.

Then, while his victim was still half-way out, Gary let go of the rope and the wheelie-bin toppled over. Our prisoner landed on the ground with a crash.

"Oh - sorry," said Gary with no pretence of regret. "My arms were getting tired."

We carried a shaken and demoralised guard into the shed.

Chapter 7

Inside the double doors was a kind of front reception centre, lit by a portable gas-lamp, where we deposited our captive on a chair and taped his arms to the back and his ankles to the chair legs.

He was a youngish man, dark, dressed in a leather jacket and jeans. There were tattoos on the backs of his hands, and he wore three gold ear-rings in one ear. He managed to look defiant and surly but definitely demoralised. He had no idea who we were or what we wanted.

"Are you the only one here?" I demanded.

"Find out for yourself," was the reply.

"Any more of that, and you go straight back in the bin," I said, and meant it. "Once again, are you on your own?"

He folded almost at once.

"Yes."

I turned to Gary.

"I'll see if I can find Miss Crawford. You stay here with our friend, and if he makes any noise or gives you the slightest trouble, tip him over backwards. His head should make a goodish hole in the floor."

"I can't wait," said Gary, who was clearly enjoying himself.

There were two rooms leading off the reception area, and I approached the first one cautiously. I had only got our captive's word that he was alone, and I was not prepared to take any chances at this late stage.

I carefully opened the door and looked round. There was another gas lamp burning on a table at one side, and two or three chairs.

On one of them, tied securely and taped across her mouth, was Emma.

Her eyes widened as she saw me, and relief was written all over her face. I quickly went over to her and gently prised the tape off her mouth.

"Thank God for that." She was at the end of her tether. I quickly cut her free from the chair.

She stood stiffly up, put her head on my shoulder and burst into tears. I held her for several moments until she recovered some of her usual poise. Eventually she broke free.

"Sorry about that," she said. "You can't imagine what it was like. They just came and put some sort of sack over my head as I was opening my front door, and bundled me inside. They kept asking me about the disc; but I didn't have it, and I knew you didn't have it – and there was nothing I could do or say that they would believe. I heard the phone-call that they made, and guessed they had you too, though what you were supposed to do about it I couldn't think. Then they blindfolded me and bundled me into a car and brought me here. They refused to say what for. I've no idea where we are. Where are we?"

"In our new factory site – the one you saw this morning. You'll be OK now." I tried to sound reassuring.

I did not remind her that the plan was to keep on cutting off her fingers if I didn't produce the disc. It didn't quite seem the moment. However, I decided I would keep fully on my guard whenever I opened my front door from now on. They obviously made a habit of striking at that particular moment.

"Come on, I'll take you out of here. But don't worry – everything is okay. For starters, I've got the disc."

A look of amazement crossed her face.

"You have? Where was it?"

"Gary Whitman had it. I've been to see him, and it's at his flat at the moment."

"Gary Whitman? I thought he hated your guts."

"I know, but he's on our side. I'll tell you about it later. At the moment he is outside keeping our ear-ringed friend in order, so don't be surprised when you see him. He's been a real help.

"I think it's time to go. I've got a van outside."

"Oh," she said, suddenly remembering something. "I think you ought to check the other room before we go. I'm not the only captive here. Someone else was brought in about an hour ago. I'm not absolutely sure who he is because I only heard him being brought in – but if he's who I think he is you may get a surprise."

I ushered her out into Reception where Gary was sitting on the desk hoping that our captive would misbehave. He and Emma acknowledged each other warily, and I opened the door to the other room.

It was a similar sized room to Emma's prison, but unlit. However, by the light from Reception I could see that there was another captive, a man, bound to a chair in the same way as Emma had been.

I wondered what to do about this other prisoner since I had no idea who he was, so I took out my torch and shone it in his face.

Nothing could have surprised me more.

"Linus!" I exclaimed. What on earth was he doing here? I removed the tape from his mouth, but decided not to cut him free until I knew what he was doing there and which side he was on.

"Why are you here?" I demanded. "Were you responsible for Miss Crawford being kidnapped?"

He looked me levelly in the eye, and said without emotion, "Aye, I'm afraid I was responsible for Miss Crawford being abducted, but not intentionally, and not in the way you think."

He spoke with a quiet authority, which I found wholly convincing.

"Go on," I said.

"I have reason to think that you and Miss Crawford have discovered the false account. But what you don't realise is that my purpose in keeping it was not for my personal gain, but to smash the whole filthy racket."

He seemed relieved to unburden himself of this information, understandably fearing for his reputation. He continued.

"I was on the point of being able to do this, but the loss of the disc had a knock-on effect which enabled them to find out that I was about to expose them. That only happened earlier this evening. That is why I was brought here, but God knows what they thought they were going to do with me. I don't think they will do anything till they have the disc."

If what he said was true, this put an entirely different slant on things. But was it true?

I decided it had to be. There was no way the gang could guess we would be able to find where they were keeping Emma, so there would be no point in planting Linus here as some sort of elaborate double-bluff on the off chance we might. Anyway, Linus was one of the most upright citizens I had ever come across, and I could well believe he would consider it his duty to expose a racket – especially if drugs were involved.

I went outside and told the others. After a short discussion, we decided to take Linus at his word and free him. We would take him with us and decide what to do next in more comfortable surroundings.

I went back to Linus and cut his bonds. He got out of the chair stiffly, thanking me.

"By the way," I said, "We've got the disc. I didn't have it – Gary Whitman did."

"Gary Whitman? How did he get it?"

"I'll tell you about it later. The thing is we've got it."

"Thank God for that," he said, relief suffusing his already florid face.

We joined the others.

"Time to go," I said. "I'm knackered."

"What are we going to do with 'im?" said Gary, nodding at our captive.

"He can stay here till we decide what to do with him. If we find the key, we will lock him in – this place is like a fortress, windows shuttered and barred, and no easy way of forcing the door. He's got water. Let him stay here and ponder the mysteries of life."

"Get stuffed," BMW Bastard said.

"How charming. Now, where's the key?"

"I took it off 'im," said Gary. "'ere it is." He produced a large bunch of keys, presumably all the keys to James' new acquisition

"Well done" I told him, and thought a moment. "I think we should have his mobile phone, too."

"I took that as well," said Gary, smugly this time.

I looked at him. "I suppose you will tell me that you removed the rags from the vent."

He looked back at me. "Well, yes - I did. They were beginning to smell awful, and you were a long time in there with Miss Crawford, so I 'ad to do something."

Gary was beginning to grow on me.

"All right, genius, do you think you can manage to open the door and we'll go."

We cut through some of our captive's bonds so that he would be able to free himself reasonably easily and walk around inside his prison after we had locked him in. Then we extinguished the gas lamps, leaving him in the dark, double-locked the steel doors and made for the BMW.

We kicked out the embers of the bonfire, and carefully locked the main gate, using the bunch of keys Gary had acquired.

"Gary, I'll drop you off at your house now, but can you come round to my flat tomorrow after breakfast? We all need some sleep now, and we must decide what we want to do, and Gary – thanks. You've been brilliant."

"Oh, come off it," he said, "You've been pretty useful yourself. P'rhaps all college boys aren't as inadequous as I'd thought."

In a spirit of mutual admiration I dropped him at his flat, but took the disc with me for safe keeping at my place. He made no objection.

I turned to my remaining passengers.

"Emma and Linus, I think you both ought to stay in my flat tonight. It would be better for you both to keep out of sight in case they saw you wandering around and guessed you had been freed. They obviously know where we all live, and may be watching. In any case, we need to talk about a number of things. My flat's got two bedrooms, so you can have one each, and I'll sleep on the sofa. We'll sort everything else out in the morning. I'm absolutely flaked."

Emma and Linus readily agreed with this suggestion, and it was with considerable relief that we entered my flat - carefully, this time - and found it exactly as I had left it.

We all had a beer and a hastily cut sandwich, and I unrolled a sleeping bag in the spare room.

We turned in almost at once, not saying a lot as we were all dead beat. Linus went straight to bed, and Emma followed almost at once. She turned in the doorway, and came back to where I was standing.

"I've never been so glad to see anyone as I was to see you tonight. I cannot stand confined spaces ever since I locked myself in the cupboard under the stairs when I was three," she said simply. "I'm glad it was you - thank you."

She kissed me firmly on the mouth, and turned into the bedroom, shutting the door behind her.

I slumped down on to the couch, and was amazed to think of all the things that had happened in the past twenty four hours. I couldn't believe it. It was less than a day since I had found Emma in my room, and since then my assessment of several people had been radically altered – Linus and Gary for a start. At least I knew who my friends were now, so that was a definite plus.

Most of all, I found myself thinking about Emma. I knew why I did have doubts about her story – after all, it did seem wholly improbable – but I felt awful about having suspected her now that I knew beyond doubt that what she had told me was true. It also meant that she had not just been buttering me up – she was genuinely concerned about the success of Mobilicity, and she did appreciate the part that I had played in that success, and had trusted me with the truth. I felt ashamed to have responded with such cynicism. I also shuddered to think what she had been through, and the terror she must have experienced at being held hostage with no apparent chance of release. The thought of bits of her fingers being chopped off one by one turned my stomach. Who were these people? What sort of animals would threaten to do a thing like that?

It had been an extraordinary day. I had been publicly praised, half-beaten up, and rescued a maiden in distress; but although I had clarified quite a lot of things in my own mind, I still didn't really know what the whole strange business was all about, or the full significance of the disc, or what we should do about it. All of those things would have to wait till the morning.

I glanced at my watch, and was amazed to find that it was only ten past twelve. Half a lifetime seemed to have passed, and tomorrow promised to be another long day.

Unsurprisingly, before I fell into an exhausted sleep, I concentrated on the look on Emma's face when she first saw me in the shed, and the moments when I was able to comfort her in my arms, and the lingering memory of her goodnight kiss.

Chapter 8

I spent a fairly uncomfortable night and woke up early with my mind still churning around the events of yesterday and mulling over the things that still had to be sorted.

I lay awake for a while and took stock. The undeniably good thing was that Emma was free and out of danger, so my greatest cause for concern had been removed. I also realised that Emma had made a bigger impression on me than I had perhaps realised. Why had I felt so protective towards her, even when she was taped up in my room? Why had I been so pleased to find out that she hadn't just been stringing me along in some seedy double cross, as at one time I had so ungallantly thought? Why had I been so upset when I realised that she really had been taken hostage, and was under imminent threat of mutilation? And why did I remember so vividly the feel of her in my arms, or that modest goodnight kiss? I suddenly knew beyond question that I wanted to see more of Emma.

I thought of some of the other girls I had known. At school I had gone round in a mixed group of friends but had not got nearer to having a regular girlfriend than a few inexpert fumblings at the school disco. At College, after a few minor experiments, I regularly went out with Tamsin, who was doing Media Studies. She was fun – a bubbly, auburn-haired girl with wide-set eyes and an infectious grin. I thought we made an impressive couple on the social scene at Brunel, such as it was, and we kept company for a couple of years. It came as something of a shock to me to realise that her ambitions seemed to centre round attracting publicity. She increasingly wanted to go clubbing in London, and as this did not particularly appeal to me – and was seriously beyond my means – she sometimes went by herself or with a couple of her girl-friends. The end really came when she ecstatically showed me one day that she appeared as a bystander in a photo in '*Hello*'. I thought that if this summarised the high point of her career so far, we probably had little in common. I didn't quite say 'For God's sake, get a life,' but she guessed my sentiments and that was that.

After I moved to Mobilicity, I had for a while teamed up with Janice, whom I met at the first Rugby Club dance after I joined. She worked for a travel agent, and had a bright and breezy nature, always knew where the modish places were for holidaying, and could get generous discounts into the bargain. She was quite fun, and came and watched a number of our matches; but I found it difficult to explain to her what it was I did. Anything in the least technical made her eyes glaze over. Now I know manufacturing does not appeal to everyone, but it happens to be one of my enthusiasms, and it would have been encouraging if she could have evinced the least bit of interest. Two months ago she had been offered a job with a sister company in Los Angeles, which she understandably accepted with alacrity. I wished her well when we said goodbye, but was less upset by her departure than I might have been. At twenty-three, I was once again a free man.

Now, I was wondering about Emma. She had a responsible and worthwhile life. I had doubted her at first, but certainly not now. She had obviously been glad that I had rescued her; but, thinking back to her comments after the staff meeting and her demeanour last night, I felt there just might be more to her response than gratitude. I hoped so. I definitely wanted to see more of her.

Next, I wondered what I should do with the disc. I did not know the full importance of it, but it clearly was of huge value to someone involved in a major drugs racket. I needed to assess what its true significance was, and also how to proceed now that it was not needed to ransom Emma. Further, I wanted to find some way of helping out Gary if it was at all possible. He was deeply and understandably concerned about the state of his brother, and I hoped it might be possible for us to find some way of helping Steve to shake off his addiction.

Then there was the question of Linus. I was sure he was on the level, but I needed to know exactly what the racket was that he said he wanted to expose, and to think how that could best be done. He would also be able to explain the full significance of the disc, and give us some idea of what we were up against.

So far, so good. These were all matters that were in our control, and we could decide what to do about.

Three things were not within our control, or needed guarding against.

The first thing that concerned me was that I was to be rung up with instructions about how to deliver the disc I was supposed to be getting hold of. It was possible that they would find out that we had rescued Emma and Linus, though I thought they probably wouldn't. They also wouldn't know whether I had traced the disc or not, but as they seemed certain I had got it, they would still be determined to retrieve it from me, hostage or no hostage. Should I say that we had rescued Emma, didn't know where the disc was, and he could get lost? I didn't think he would believe me. Should I say I had the disc, but demand some cash to be used for Gary's brother? Or should I agree that I had the disc, and give it to him as he requested, but tell the police and have him arrested with it?

I thought it would be better not to disclose that we had rescued Emma and Linus. The fact that they were no longer hostages gave us the whip hand, and I knew we had to keep whatever slender advantages we possessed. Our opponents clearly knew where Emma and Linus lived, and for all I knew they might be watching or even searching their homes. One thing was certain. If any of their gang saw Emma or Linus openly walking about on this Saturday morning, it might drive them to desperate measures. I had no doubt that they were prepared to be as ruthless as necessary to get the disc back, and I was not going to let anyone else on our side get hurt. They had done enough already.

The final unwelcome possibility was that Mr Big would try to contact his crony shut up in the factory. He would get no answer, of course, because we had his mobile, so he might possibly check up on the building in person. If he discovered what had happened, that might also provoke them into desperate measures, and we would have no warning of it. However, I consoled myself with the thought that Mr Big had indicated that there was to be a minimum of contact between him and Emma's captor; and in any case we might be able to switch on the captured mobile to see if there were any messages. We'd have to see when Gary brought it later.

I eventually got up, washed and shaved, and then clattered around getting some tea and breakfast things on the table.

Emma emerged looking rather more relaxed than the night before, said "Hi", and disappeared into the bathroom.

Linus emerged, radiating grimness.

"I've been thinking to myself how I must have seemed to you," he said matter-of-factly. "You must have thought I was a complete villain. Thank you for believing me. I told you the truth."

"I'm sure you did and you're right – we both thought you were leading a major racket, though we had no idea what. Sorry I distrusted you."

He seemed mollified, but only a little.

Emma joined us, her hair down, but still in her light blue suit of yesterday. It was, of course, the only outfit she had available, and looked a bit crumpled after the excitements of the night before.

"Morning, Oliver, morning, Linus. I could murder a cup of that tea."

I poured her a large mugful, and put some bread in the toaster. We all settled down to breakfast, not quite knowing where to begin. I thought it would be best to start out with Linus.

"How did you get into this, Linus?" I asked him directly.

He seemed relieved to be able to clear up his position.

"It all began over two years ago when my mother died. She and my father had moved down from Scotland to be near me when they retired, and her death hit my father very hard. She died from a stroke, and he was not expecting it.

"My father tried to cope with his bereavement by getting out a bit. He had always been a keen golfer, and had joined a club locally, though he had not spent much time there before my mother's death. He was a typical Scot – didn't say much, didn't confide in other people, kept his feelings to himself. I'm the same."

"My father was Low Church, very straight-laced and moral, but he had only one vice, which was smoking. He smoked a lot after my mother died, and he obviously smoked at the Golf Club.

"As I understand it, one day he fell into conversation with a member there, and said he was feeling down. He was offered a cigarette which, he was told would 'make him feel better'. It did. It made him feel a lot better, and he was given a packet of them."

"My father had no knowledge of drugs, and had made it a strict rule of life to have nothing to do with them. He didn't realise what he was doing, and it only took a week or so before he couldn't do without them. The cost started to go up, but there was nothing he could do about it."

"At first, he didn't understand what was happening – he had no experience of drugs or users or pushers. Then he saw a programme about drug abuse on the television, and he finally realised that he had become an addict."

"It devastated him. There he was, a Calvinist to the core, who had become a drug addict. He had always thought addicts were weak-character'd or downright immoral people, and the fact that he had become one was too much for him to bear."

Linus stopped, and it took Spartan discipline for him to withhold tears.

"What did he do?" asked Emma gently.

Linus pulled himself together.

"He went up to St Andrews, played a round of golf, returned to his hotel and threw himself off a fifth storey balcony. He sent me a letter apologising."

There was a long silence. Both Emma and I felt Linus' obvious pain, but neither of us quite knew how to express our sympathy. He understood our silence.

"It gets worse," he said after a while. "After the funeral, I was approached by a well-dressed man who claimed he was a fellow-member of my father's Club, and knew my father well. He also said that my father owed him twenty three thousand pounds. I simply couldn't believe it.

"I asked him what this was for, and he said for goods supplied. I asked him for invoices and so on, but he replied that there were no invoices for the goods in question, and that it was a debt of honour."

"I insisted on knowing more, but he turned aggressive and said that unless I paid the amount he demanded, he would make it known throughout the Club and beyond that my father was an addict and left unpaid debts. My father was a proud man, and so am I. He knew I could not allow my father or my family to be thought of in that way."

"However, he said there was an alternative. He knew I was the Accounts Director of a manufacturing company, and that if I would cooperate with him in setting up a special account, sited overseas, in the company's name, and use it for his purposes, he would forget about the debt and my father's reputation."

"I knew perfectly well what he wanted me to do – launder the money from his drug-trafficking. I was about to tell him to go to hell when I thought that if I could manage his drugs account for a time, keeping exact details of every transaction, I might be able to expose him and his filthy racket for good. So, I pretended to go along with his suggestion so that I could bring him to some sort of justice for what he had done to my father."

"How exactly did the system work?" asked Emma, her professional interest aroused.

"Och, it was quite a clever scheme," answered Linus, professional to professional. "We opened a special account in Mobilicity's name overseas, in a place where fewer questions are asked and secrecy is expected. Obviously, checks were made, but Mobilicity is a properly registered company, and it was easy to establish that I was a company official. The account was kept entirely separate from all the rest of Mobilicity's business. I was the only one in the company who knew of it, and who had access to it.

"The account needed two signatures, mine and someone else's, so that was how we did it. Money – usually cash – could be paid in and then paid out as bona fide money from a bona fide account. Thus illicit money from drugs could be re-cycled and be paid out as legitimate money from a respectable firm. This is a successful scam, but can only last for a short time to be safe."

"Yes," said Emma. "The tax authorities would begin to cross reference any cheques you paid out, and official questions would be asked. As soon as anyone tried to tie up those cheques with the official Mobilicity accounts they would smell a rat."

Linus nodded. "Exactly."

"But when I was doing the audit, there was no way I could have found your special account. There were simply no figures that could indicate it," Emma insisted.

"Of course not," Linus agreed. "An audit would not pick it up. But the Revenue would get a line on it sooner or later. That is why we were just about to close the account and transfer the cash to a new special account, and repeat the process with another bank. I was just about to pay in the final cash payment before doing this."

"I don't quite see where the disc comes in," I said.

"Ah," he went on, "That is the cunning bit. As a matter of principle, I kept all the transactions for that account on the single disc. It was too dangerous having a number of different copies, or leaving it on the computer, or having print-outs. Therefore everything to do with the account was on the one disc. What's more, it was a very special disc"

"What was so special about it?" I asked.

"It was a CD-PRONC."

"What the hell's that?"

"Not many people know about them," said Linus patiently. "I think they are being developed for the music and e-book industry to prevent pirating. It stands for Compact Disc Password Read Only Non Copyable, and does what it says. It requires a password to read it, cannot be altered, and has a device to prevent the disc being copied. You can add to it, but you can't erase anything. It is considered to be as secure as a disc can ever be.

"I have been recording every transaction in and out for the past year. The entire account is on that disc, on that disc only, and it is not capable of being transferred anywhere else. That's why it is so important – the whole racket appears on that single disc and on that alone."

It was obvious why a multi-million drugs trafficker would want to keep control of it. I began to fear that our opponents might be more desperate than I had thought.

"Unfortunately, that's not all," Linus continued.

"I did as I was asked, and kept the records as required on the first part of the disc which was simply paying in anonymous amounts, and paying out cheques mostly to bogus companies. But also, further down the disc, not visible unless you scroll down a long way, I secretly kept a list of names and details about all the people paying in and particularly of those to whom we were paying out, because those were the people supplying the stuff in the first place. It was mostly crack."

"Every so often they would check up on the accounts, which I would put up on the screen, and everything was absolutely correct. They were impressed, and began to trust me. Of course, I did not show them the list further down – why should they suspect it was there?"

We sat silently, totally absorbed in Linus' story.

"Then came Friday – yesterday. I had been told that they wanted to have a final check on the disc because they had decided to close the account and transfer it somewhere else. I knew this was likely to happen, and had been checking it over on Thursday when I was stung by that wasp."

"Yes," said Emma, "That's when I saw it. I couldn't believe fifteen million."

"I'm sure you couldn't, you just having audited the proper accounts." Linus could imagine the amazement of a fellow professional.

"Before I left for hospital, I took out the disc and left it amongst the others – the most natural place for it, where I fully expected it to be when I came back on Friday.

"You can imagine my concern when I found it wasn't there. I was supposed to be having a final closing down session, and I had to tell them that the disc had been stolen. They went absolutely berserk. I was in a panic to get it back, and then I thought of checking the CCTV. I was quite unprepared to see you and Miss Crawford sneaking in to my office in the middle of the night. I thought it had to be you who had taken it."

"Yes," I said. "We must have looked highly suspicious. Unfortunately, we didn't find it."

"No, but you can see why I assumed you had it, though I could not guess why. I hadn't got any time to make up a story to explain its absence. They became very insistent, threatening all sorts of things. In the end I had to tell them what had happened. They said they would sort it out with you, and promised that there would be no violence, believing that you must have taken the disc by mistake. They made me find out from the office where you both lived. I now realise what for, but I didn't then.

"Later on, they told me they were going to kidnap Miss Crawford as a hostage for the safe return of the disc, and could I suggest a safe place to keep her. It was very difficult to think of anywhere until I remembered the unused factory site, for which we fortunately had the keys. I thought it would be ideal as it would be well out of the way and deserted over the weekend. So I gave them the keys, which would not be missed if I put them back on Monday."

He looked at Emma. "I really had no idea they were going to treat you so roughly. I'm so sorry."

"Can't be helped," said Emma. "I'd probably have done the same."

We sat silent for a moment, understanding the plight that our dour colleague had got himself into.

"How did you get thrown in with Emma?" I asked suddenly.

Linus sagged at the memory.

"That's the worst bit," he sighed. "When I started out on this scheme, it was with the sole intention of exposing it. The more I see of it, the more I think it should be exposed. These people are poison."

"However, I was afraid that if I was doing their work for them I might be accused of being one of the gang, and so I had to give myself some protection. What I did was to write a full account of my intentions, and outline the scheme and my motives in undertaking it. I made two copies, sealed them up, and got a bank and a solicitor each to keep a copy for me, witnessing the date on the outside, and to be released either to me on demand, or opened at my death."

"Very sensible precaution, in the circumstances," I commented.

"Yes, you would think so," he continued. "Unfortunately, they had become jumpy about me and the disc, and began asking around. One of the people they happened to ask, on an old boy basis at a golf club, I understand, was the solicitor with whom I had lodged my statement. He let it be known that I had lodged a very unusual document with him."

"But it would have been entirely unprofessional to open your document," Emma protested.

"Yes," said Linus. "It would. Unfortunately, the solicitor in question depended upon them for his supply of crack. He did as he was told."

"That's awful," I said, just beginning to realise the position he was in.

Linus' body language remained uneasy. "It's worse than awful, because they now know that I am the one person who can blow open their racket, and have every intention of doing so. They were not pleased. They grabbed me at my house, bundled me into a car, and threw me in to the shed at the factory, where you found me."

"I have no idea what they intend to do with me. Fortunately, they need my signature to finalise the present account, though I suppose they could attempt to forge it. They threatened to implicate me fully if anything I did resulted in their downfall since they thought my alibi had been removed by destroying my explanation. It was just as well I kept quiet about the other letter at the bank.

"They were livid to think that I had been using my time to build evidence against them, and it will get worse if they find out I have all the names on the disc. I'm not their favourite person."

"The strange thing is they cannot access their account without me and the disc. They must feel safe for the moment because they have no idea I can get at the disc which I would need to expose them. But you can see why they want it."

I could see only too well, and I shuddered to think what they would do to Linus once they had got the disc and cleared their account. He would inevitably be seen as an unacceptable threat. I needed to know more.

"Linus, you keep referring to 'they'. Who exactly are 'they'?"

He pondered for a moment.

"I don't know all of them but there are several. The one I have had most to do with, and who appears to be their leader, is called Russell Deverell."

"Who's he?"

"I would put him down as a public school type gone wrong – a Flashman or a Steerforth.

"He's in his mid-thirties, and appears a real charmer on the surface. He has exemplary manners, and the right accent, background and image. He naturally fits into the club world. He probably has money of his own, but chooses to use it to make what he considers easy money in large amounts."

"Beneath this urbane front, he is a total bastard. He is completely amoral and utterly ruthless. He thinks easy money is his right, considers himself above the law, and despises the addicts whose addiction he promotes. Naturally he recruits his pushers from people he has manoeuvred into dependency, so they destroy themselves and take the risk while he demands the profit. In my opinion, he is pure evil." Linus spoke these last words with a new level of intensity.

I had to agree with him. It was one thing to hear about stories like this in theory; but when I thought of Steve Whitman, I could see only too well what the results were in practice.

I also guessed that it was Russell Deverell who had collared me last night. I felt I had a score to settle with him.

At that moment, there was a knock on the door. I opened it suspiciously, but quickly let in Gary and a person I assumed to be his brother.

Chapter 9

"This is my brother Steve," announced Gary, somewhat unnecessarily.

The likeness was unmistakable. He was rather smaller, but had the same spare stature, sandy hair and blue eyes, and differed only in two respects. He had the nervous twitch and waxen skin of a junkie which accentuated the sunken features of his face. On the other hand, the dark-circled eyes hid a mixture of intelligence and desperation which immediately made me feel for him. I thought what a waste of a human being.

"Steve's got some news," said Gary.

He had our full attention.

"Well," he started hesitantly, not sure about us, even though I guessed Gary had briefed him fully. "There's two things. First up, they are very edgy about something. They've been questioning all their contacts, and threatening they will cut off the supply if they step out of line. They haven't tried to make me, like, do anything yet, but if they did I'd have no choice. I have to have their stuff, and they've, like, cornered the market locally. To have my supply cut off is not an option. You mightn't rate this, but you just gotta believe me. You also gotta believe they have the same hold on loads of other people. They can make us do anything they want."

"Next, they are demanding more from me. I've gotta go and recruit more contacts, and demand more from those I already got. It's full time hassle, and they'll go on demanding more and more until I break or get caught."

"That's why I gotta get out. I know I've been a fool, but at least I've realised it; and I would be a total crackhead if I didn't try to do something about it. Gary has been trying to help, but he hasn't got the money to get me a proper detox. If you can help, it would, like, save my life, because I won't go on like this. I'll end up like all the others, Brahms and Boracic." He lapsed into his own world.

Emma and I looked at each other. We shook our heads.

I said to Gary, "Sorry, he lost me. Brahms and Boracic?"

He shrugged. "Street slang. Brahms and Liszt – pissed. Boracic lint – skint."

Steve had spoken in earnest desperation. I was really sorry for him, and could quite see the pressure Gary felt to do something for his brother.

Linus broke the silence. "I know exactly how you feel, Steve. My father killed himself for much the same reason. This is why I am attempting to smash the whole corrupt lot of them."

"I've told Steve," said Gary, "and we'll both do anything we can to 'elp."

"That's excellent," I said warmly, "Welcome to the club, Steve. If we can smash them once and for all, I'm sure we will be able to fix up the detox part for you. You have my word."

"Cool," said Steve. "Anything."

Linus interposed, "I think I might be able to help there. I'll tell you about it later."

"For the moment, though," I continued, "it is important that they don't connect Gary and you with us. They don't know Gary had the disc, and they don't know you are in with us. It would be very awkward if they found out either of those things.

"So, Gary and Steve, you go home and stay there. Do whatever you usually do, but keep within phoning distance. By the way, Gary, did you bring the mobile you took off our friend? If they made any calls it might give us a clue what they would do next."

"Yeah, I looked at it, but it was switched off, and I don't know the PIN number so I can't regurgitate it. Sorry."

"Can't be helped. Anyway, you go back to your flat, and I'll keep you informed. We need to keep in touch, but one of our main strengths is that the opposition don't know we are on the same side. If you need to talk, ring me on my mobile."

I gave him my number, and checked carefully that my flat was not under surveillance before letting them out. The two brothers drove off without fuss.

"I felt so sorry for both of them," said Emma reflectively. "I hope there's something we can do."

"There is," said Linus.

"Go on."

"Well, I told you that I was supposed to be closing the account, but I hadn't made the final payment. What usually happens is that I collect a number of payments and pay them in as a large lump sum. At the moment I have about twenty seven thousand pounds sitting in a bag in a safe deposit in a bank. It is completely untraceable, being the proceeds of a few weeks drug trading. The point is if we can break the gang and show up their account, nobody but me will know that the final payment was not made. I think it should be devoted to a suitable good cause. I can think of one."

"Linus, that's brilliant," I said.

"And very appropriate," pointed out Emma. "Drug money to help re-establish a drugs victim. Couldn't be better."

I enjoyed sharing a moment of euphoria, but knew we had to clear the decks and get back to some serious business.

We had finished breakfast, and while Linus was borrowing my shaving equipment in the bathroom, Emma and I shared the washing up in my kitchen. It seemed an agreeably domestic experience.

"Why did you let them go like that?" asked Emma. "I thought we might be acting together in this."

"We are, but at the moment we cannot risk the enemy knowing they are in it with us. They don't know that Gary took the disc, or that we have it, or that Steve can help us in a number of ways. Steve said they have control of all sorts of people, and we can't have him being identified as part of our outfit. To be brutally frank, if they refused to supply Steve with his fix, he would do anything they ordered him to. You heard what he said."

"Like Linus said, it's a filthy racket," said Emma with feeling, drying up the spoons. "How far away does Gary live?"

"He has a flat on Rodborough hill, just off the Common. Do you know it?"

"Rodborough Common? Isn't that where the ice-cream place is?"

"Yes, that's right. Winstone's. Why?"

"It's my favourite ice cream – well, their rum and raisin is, double cornet and no flake. Our family used to go for walks on the common, and we always ended up there."

"Where do you come from, Emma? You can't be far away."

"Well, my family come from Cheltenham, but I've got a small flat in Birdlip. When I left college and decided to go in for accountancy, I thought I'd better get on the housing ladder as soon as possible. My parents helped out to get me started."

"I want to do that, too," I agreed. "I'm renting this at the moment, but hope to buy something as soon as I've paid off my student loan. Fortunately, that shouldn't be too long."

A thought occurred to me. "By the way, do you have a mobile? I think it would be sensible if we could reach each other, just in case."

We swapped numbers, and to be on the safe side I posted it into my mobile's memory under 'E'.

I was secretly pleased to know that Emma was within easy reach, and hoped that we would be able to get to know each other better when all this drugs business had been sorted.

The washing up complete, we rejoined Linus in the sitting room.

"Right," I said, "We've got two or two and a half hours to decide what we are going to do. "Option One is to wait for the call, do what we are told about delivering the disc, and simply let them have it. Comments?"

"Absolutely not," said Emma immediately. That would mean Linus here would be at their mercy, Steve would have no chance of breaking free, and there would be no chance of paying for a detox. We cannot let those things happen. This lot has to be exposed and broken up. We have no choice."

I was heartened by Emma's decisive response, which exactly reflected my own sentiments.

"Linus?"

"I know it is in my own selfish interests not to allow them to win, and I might well have to suffer for it now they know where I stand. I also know that it's likely to be very dangerous to cross them, and I don't want anyone else getting hurt on my behalf. That said, I can only admire the unambiguous response of Miss Crawford – may I call you Emma? – I would like to think we should do everything in our power to stop them. It was my original purpose, and I certainly don't want to give up now and let them get away with it."

"In that case, we all agree."

"Option Two. We wait till the call comes, but decide to set some sort of a trap for them. The trouble is, we don't know their strength, and we don't know what we shall be told to do. We'll have to make plans on the hoof after I have been told what to do with the disc. It all seems a bit chancy."

There was a pause, and then Emma spoke.

"There is a third option. I have an uncle who is in the police. The narcotics section. We could ask him for some advice, and possibly some back-up."

"Emma, that's brilliant. Can you reach him - like now? It would certainly give us some professional help. Oh," I thought of something. "We'd have to make sure we don't let him run in Linus and Steve. I shouldn't want that."

"I know, that's why I didn't mention it before. But if you are determined to smash this lot, I believe he is our best bet. I have been thinking what I would say to him, and you'll have to trust me to explain everything. I'm sure Linus will be all right with his remaining letter, but I cannot be absolutely certain about Steve. He is a pusher, after all."

"Aye, but he's under duress," said Linus. "I'm sure they would take that into account, and the fact that he's helping us. I have no doubt that, if he were here, he would want us to call in your uncle."

Emma said that was fine, and rang him. She gave a brilliantly concise account of the position, and within five minutes her uncle had agreed to come to my flat in the time it took to drive from Cheltenham to my flat in Paganhill. He sounded really keen to get into action.

"This money laundering," I said. "How exactly does it work?"

"To begin with," said Linus, "You need to have someone with a lot of illegal cash to deal with. Very often it is drug money, but it can be from prostitution or illegal gambling. If people have large amounts of actual cash about them they get nervous."

"Why is that?" I queried.

"Because it attracts attention. Either you make yourself a target for others who try to take it off you – and the more you have the harder they'll try – or the law begins to notice. Either way, it is much better if it can be put into a safe legitimate account somewhere, from which it can be withdrawn in a normal manner."

"But the trouble must come in finding a suitable account," said Emma.

"Exactly," Linus continued. "You either have to have a crooked bank, or a crooked firm, or a crooked accountant in a legitimate firm. It is difficult for banks to get away with blatant laundering, and so often a bogus company is set up. The trouble with this is that it has to file its name on the Companies Register, which means it has to submit annual accounts. Any company which simply had money coming in and going out would immediately attract suspicion, and if it tried to hide large amounts of money amongst its other trading activities it would be bound to show up when the accounts were audited."

"That's why I was so concerned when I first saw that disc," said Emma. "All the figures added up and could be properly accounted for. When I suddenly saw a fifteen million bottom line on Mobilicity-headed paper I couldn't believe it."

"No," agreed Linus, "and if you had not seen the other disc you would never have known. That is the cleverest way of laundering money on that scale – but it needs someone like me to do it. I set up an account in a legitimate company's name, but keep all the illegal money separate. It is an account at a separate bank, which can verify my credentials; it has separate signatures on separate cheque books, and a completely separate set of books. Providing there is no leak, the illegal account can go on operating while the legitimate part of the business can be audited till the cows come home, and nothing will appear wrong.

"There are only two problems with this system. The first is when someone accidentally mixes up the two accounts – for example, if a cheque drawn on the illegal account was sent back to the company, and it was seen by someone other than the bent accountant. There would be no reference to it anywhere, and questions would be asked. If you, Emma, had tried to audit a cheque drawn on a Mobilicity account for which you could find no cheque-book, or account reference, you would immediately have been suspicious."

"I certainly would. I may not be a fully qualified accountant yet, but there is no way I could have missed that."

"I'm sure you wouldn't. The second problem comes after a while. Some cheques will be issued on the dud account, and of course they will be honoured. Unfortunately, the source of the credit will eventually appear in someone's tax return, and eventually one of these cheques will be cross-referred. In other words, the Revenue will go back to the source of the cheque, and will find that there is no reference to it in the legitimate books. That is why Russell was changing this account. He had not been rumbled so far, but was taking no chances. If he was later challenged, there would be no account against which his past operations could be checked."

"Are those the only ways money can be laundered?" I asked.

"Oh no, there's all sorts of ways. Betting shops, fairgrounds, casinos and so on for smaller sums – anywhere that ready cash changes hands. But for serious amounts of money, it is necessary to work out something with a bank account, unless you don't mind having a garage full of used notes to look after."

I never realised the lengths to which people obviously went to disguise their ill-gotten gains.

We spent the next few minutes reviewing the whole position, delighted with what we had done so far but a little apprehensive about what was to follow. We felt sure that we had the initiative at the moment, but we could lose that as soon as they discovered the real position. I was particularly concerned to learn just how big an operation we had become involved in, and guessed that our opponents would have considerable resources at their disposal. I also guessed they would not hesitate to take whatever steps were necessary to retrieve their disc since it was obviously so important to them.

I knew we needed some professional support if we were not to be submerged in an operation which was outside our experience.

After a short forty minutes, there was a knock on the door and Emma's uncle arrived. He introduced himself as Detective Inspector James Crawford, and was involved in the whole anti-drugs scene throughout the South Cotswolds. Emma knew him as Uncle Jim, and this somehow seemed to suit him. He was in his forties, dark haired and quite tall, dressed in typical Saturday morning casual clothes. I liked him.

"As soon as Emma told me I guessed what you had stumbled into," he said earnestly. "I suppose you don't have a name?"

"How does Russell Deverell sound?" I asked.

"It sounds a bit on the dangerous side. We have been trying to nail him for a long time, but he is difficult to pin down. What do you have on him?"

Emma and I explained about the events of the previous couple of days, and Linus filled in the background to the disc. Uncle Jim seemed excited by the news.

"And you have this disc now?" he asked.

"Yes, it's on the desk over there," I said, pointing. "No doubt Linus will put it up on the screen if that would help."

"It won't compromise me, will it?" said Linus

"You have my word," said Uncle Jim. "Even without your sealed letter of intent, I can promise you if you can help us smash this lot we shall all be in your debt."

Reassured, Linus put the disc into my PC and entered the password. Immediately there showed up the main account which had so surprised Emma on Thursday. What was even more surprising was that these were the figures for less than a year. We were into serious money here.

However, it was the lists right down at the end of the disc that really engaged Uncle Jim's interest. As the names scrolled by, he several times exclaimed in delight.

"Good Lord, so that's where it comes from."

"Yes, I knew he'd be in there somewhere."

"I'd never have believed it of him."

He was in a professional world of his own. He couldn't believe the damning evidence he had at his disposal, and said so.

"You all realise that this is absolute dynamite? We could never have collected information as good as this in a month of Sundays. I'm not surprised they want it back."

He paused for a moment.

"Will you let me keep this? I think it ought to remain secure, and will be of vital use in sorting these creatures out. However, it is important that we get our friend Russell Deverell. I notice his name does not appear anywhere on these lists, and so our only chance of putting him away will be to catch him at it.

"Therefore, when he rings up and gives you your instructions, tell him that you have been able to locate the disc, but stall for time. Agree to what he wants, but tell him that you can't get at it at the moment. Tell him that you will comply with all his requests, but it will have to wait till tomorrow. Ask him to reassure you that Emma will be safe till then so as not to arouse his suspicion.

"A lot will depend on how you handle this call. Do you think you will manage it all right?"

"Yes, I think so." I gulped

"Of course he can," said Emma displaying more confidence than I felt.

"If that goes all right," continued Uncle Jim, "It will give us some time to bring in some professional back-up and lay a proper trap. I know some of my lads won't mind losing part of their weekend to get Russell D. We've been after him for ages."

I liked the idea of professional back-up, and it was comforting to have the gravitas and experience of Uncle Jim taking control. I had increasingly begun to feel that we were getting out of our depth, and when I heard the full extent of the racket which the disc demonstrated I realised the full weight of crooked interests that would be ranged against us.

"What do we do now?" Emma asked.

"We sit and wait for the call. Do you have any other suggestions?"

We didn't, so we sat and waited.

It was quarter past eleven.

Chapter 10

It has always amazed me how slowly time goes when waiting for something important to happen, and this was no exception. I made some coffee for everyone, and while we sat around Uncle Jim asked Linus if he could give any more information about any of the people in the racket.

"I can't, to tell you the truth," he replied. "It was just the one man, Russell Deverell that I saw. Of course, he mentioned other people in a general way, but I never met them. I could tell you quite a lot about him, though."

He repeated the description he had given me.

Uncle Jim nodded. "That's typical. There are usually two or three big collaborators at the top, but they operate as individuals. Most of them get the dirty work done by people dependent on them, so they never have to show themselves except to a very few trusted people. It is rather like pyramid selling; the risk is transferred down, while the profits go to the top. It is only through finding where the profits go to that leads us to the ringleaders. That's why this disc is so important, together with the fact that it helps us to discover where the stuff is coming from. That gives us a chance to intercept the supply chain."

"Will it shut them down for good?" I asked.

"Well, if we can catch them and make the charges stick, then yes, it will – until another operator comes along to fill the gap. If the demand is there, another supply route will always be found – that is why it is a constant battle for us in the narcotics squad."

"So it makes no difference if they are caught?" Linus seemed mystified.

"Oh yes, it makes a difference to them," Uncle Jim explained. "If we can show that drug pushing is a serious risk, it might deter some people. If pushers simply got away with making huge profits from drugs, every villain in town would be at it."

That certainly made sense, and I had to admit that the thought of Russell Deverell being in gaol for a long stretch appealed to me a great deal.

I thought it best to bring up the question of Steve Whitman. I told him the story as Gary had given it to me, and said that both he and Steve were willing to do anything to help us smash this particular gang.

Uncle Jim looked solemn. "I wonder how many times I've heard of people in that position before," he sighed. "They always think they can handle it, and it's only when they find they can't that they realise it is impossible to give up. Some people estimate that as much as half the crime in the country is carried out to feed a habit which people can't afford and often want to break."

"What do they do?" asked Emma.

"Whatever's necessary," replied her uncle. "Some of them become pushers, and get their own supply and some of the profits. Some of them cheat, and cut the stuff with any additive they can get away with to bulk it out and make more money – flour, talcum powder, you wouldn't believe it. At the bottom of the pile are the poor sods who have to have their fix, but can't get the money legally, so they go in for petty thieving or prostitution. That's how almost all of the petty thieves, rent boys and ladies of the night got started in the first place. Once there, they can't escape until they die, or get caught and cleaned up. Even then, many go back. They can't do anything else."

"Well, what about Steve?" I persisted.

There was a pause. "I don't know how much stuff he has pushed, but I do know this. If he really wants to kick the habit – and it certainly won't be easy – it would be better to have him clean than send him to gaol. He would not only come out with a record, which would make it harder to get a job, but would almost certainly get in with a druggy lot in prison, and go straight back on it when he comes out."

"Wouldn't he get sorted out while in prison?" asked Emma.

She was treated to a pitying look by her uncle.

"Many of the prisons almost run on drugs," he said. "Of course there are various schemes for treating addiction. At a crude guess, I would say they attract about one tenth of the resources that are required. The simple fact is many inmates come out worse than they went in. As far as drugs are concerned, they don't know better, they just know more.

"Anyway, back to your friend Steve. If he really can help us, and if I am convinced that he really does want to quit, and if I know that he can go on a good rehab scheme somewhere, then I have no doubt that both he and society would be better off if he did not go to prison. I have considerable discretion about who is and is not prosecuted; and if he has not been spinning you a web of lies then I would not want him sent down."

"That's a lot of 'ifs' " I commented.

"There have to be. Addicts are very persuasive and very plausible. They have to learn how to con money out of people, and they quickly find out what people want to hear from them, and then say whatever it is they wish to know. The truth has nothing to do with it. Like your alcoholic, the addict learns all the tricks of the trade to convince both himself and you of whatever he needs to get the next drink or the next fix. You wouldn't believe the stories I've heard – all of them lies. That's what makes it so difficult for those who genuinely want to reform, because it is too easy to believe that their most earnest protestations are just more ingratiating lies. I'm sorry to sound so cynical about human nature, but so would you be if you had been in this sort of work as long as I have."

He paused for a moment.

"However, I can promise you this. I've had enough experience of these characters to make a reasonable guess as to whether they are genuine or not, and if they have the determination to come off drugs. I'll certainly assess Steve informally, and if he is as you hope then I will do all I can to help in his rehabilitation. Did you say you could get him into a proper detox centre?"

"Yes, I can," said Linus tersely, not wanting to divulge the nature of the funding for this enterprise.

"Good," said Uncle Jim, and we left it there. I thought Steve would get as good a deal as he was likely to be offered anywhere else.

The time dragged by.

At ten past twelve the phone rang.

Nerves a-jangle, I picked it up.

A recorded voice said, "Congratulations, your household has been selected from your area to qualify for a …."

I slammed the phone down in disgust. What I was depriving myself of I never knew, but I didn't want it anyway.

There was a tense silence in the room, and I went over various ploys I might try to buy the time I was told we needed. One difficulty was that I might not have the choice. If I was just played a recorded message, like the stupid phone-sales call I had just received, I would not be able to stall. I would just have to do what I was told, and it might be difficult to arrange a delayed exchange. Alternatively, I might have to give it to them in some complicated way, which would make it difficult to catch him in possession.

At exactly twelve thirty, the phone rang again.

"Is that Oliver Howson?"

"Yes,"

"Are you alone?"

"Yes," I lied.

"Good. You have my disc?"

"Yes and no. I told you I didn't have it, and I didn't. However, I have managed to find out where it is."

"Good," the voice on the phone purred. "I somehow felt you would."

"Look, you smug prat, you don't recognise the truth when it jumps out in front of you. I had no idea where it was, and it was only by sheer luck that I traced it."

"Tut, tut, the gentleman seems annoyed." I could hear him smirking down the phone. "This is what I want you to do to get it back to me. You are…"

"Wait a minute," I almost shouted. "I said I knew where it was. I didn't say I had it."

This clearly threw him. My manner had convinced him that I was a straight talking sort of person, and he was wondering how to play it. I used his indecision to ram home my point.

"I am sure I can get it, but there is no way that I can get hold of it before tomorrow morning. You have to believe that there is nothing I can do to get it before then. It would just be impossible."

"You can get it then?"

"Yes, I am sure I can. But I need from you an absolute assurance that Miss Crawford will not be harmed in any way. If she is made to suffer at all for a delay which I cannot help, then I shall destroy the disc and whatever's on it as soon as I get it."

I knew perfectly well that any promise he made could be entirely empty, but there was just sufficient weight in my threat to give him pause. The thought that I might destroy the disc hadn't occurred to him. He had no idea I knew just how important it was for him.

He decided to be ingratiating.

"My dear chap, don't get so het up. This is purely a business deal, and I would prefer to conduct it on gentlemanly lines. We both have something the other wants. I'm sure we can arrange a fair exchange without any unpleasantness. I will certainly return your goods undamaged in any way if you will agree to return mine in the same condition. I have absolutely no wish to harm Miss Crawford – not unless it becomes necessary. However, as soon as you return the disc, I can give you my word it will not be necessary."

I felt I had got my way.

"All right, I agree. I should have the disc in my possession by about midday."

"Very good. This is what I want you to do. Do you know a restaurant called the Egypt Mill at Nailsworth?"

"Yes," I said, "Why?"

"I will reserve a table in your name on the ground floor restaurant for lunchtime tomorrow. Twelve thirty. Do you have a Waitrose plastic bag?"

"Yes," I said, surprised.

"Good. Put the disc in the bag and take it in with you. Have a reasonably quick lunch, and leave the bag when you go. I will reserve the same table for one-fifteen, and pick up the bag, which you have left. Our table will be up a few steps and near to a window, so you can leave the bag on the sill by the table. No-one will notice it there, especially as I will follow you directly. You will go straight home. I will examine the disc, and if it is all correct you will have a message on your answerphone telling you where Miss Crawford can be found. If you do as I say, I can assure you of her safety."

Great, I thought, that means you get your disc, and I get Emma only if you wish to lose a hostage. However, I decided to pretend it sounded a fair deal.

"All right, I accept. I should be able to collect the disc and be there by about half twelve, but I may be a moment or two late, so don't panic. You've given me your word, so I'll give you mine. I'll be there."

"I'm sure you will," he said smoothly. "We'll be watching for you."

He hung up.

"Well done," said Uncle Jim, grinning. "I haven't heard such a convincing load of old tosh for a long time. I particularly liked the warning that you might be a little late, so don't worry – very artistic. It makes it sound as though you might have to rush there after collecting the disc – it's just as well he doesn't know you had it all the time and the bit about giving him your word was very gentlemanly."

"Well, I will be there. I wouldn't miss catching the bastard for anything," I replied. "Anyway, that gives us some time to form a plan. Over to you."

Uncle Jim looked seriously at me for several seconds.

"Are you sure you want to go along with this drop? You don't have to, you know. We have probably got enough to convict him as it is – but it if we could actually catch him in possession of the disc it would be the icing on the cake."

It hadn't occurred to me that I had the option. I wanted to see this through.

"I don't see why not. Our friend Russell deserves to be put away and I owe him one after what he did to me, and threatened to do to Emma. Yes, I'd like to. After all, your men will be right there if anything went wrong. I don't see there is a problem."

Uncle Jim looked approving.

"At least we know where the hand-over is to be, so that's one thing out of the way. Also, lunchtime tomorrow will give me plenty of scope to set a trap for our friend. He let it be known that you will be watched, so it means that we will have to have a succession of our people coming in and out before and during the operation. It would be a bit obvious having three or four plainclothes men in boots leaning up against the bar even if they aren't expecting us."

He got up from his chair.

"I'll leave you now, and go back and sort out my men for tomorrow. I will arrange for a casual rota of my men to come and go from twelve o'clock onwards, and it looks as though he will be doing something of the same sort – that should be fun. However, they will simply be looking out for you, whereas we will be after much bigger game. I would like Linus to come with me and bring the disc. He will be able to help us analyse the figures, and we will be able to take all the necessary information we need."

"But I thought it couldn't be copied," I said.

"Well, it can't in normal circumstances. However, some of our whiz kids can do all sorts of funny things with discs, believe me. As a last resort, we could capture the screen image, but I hope that won't be necessary. Whatever else happens, we will have the information, and I will bring the disc back to you so that you can put it into the Waitrose bag."

"What? We're not actually giving the thing back to him?" I said, startled.

"Of course," Uncle Jim replied. "That's the whole point. Ideally, we need to catch him with it in his possession. That is effectively the only way we can incontestably tie him in to the racket. Anyway, we will get the disc back when he is arrested."

Thinking about it, I saw he was right.

Uncle Jim left, taking Linus and the disc with him, promising to bring the disc back in the morning. He would then be able to fill me in with the details of the plans for Sunday lunch, and what would happen after.

He thought it better if Linus remained with his squad to brief them as fully as possible on all he knew about the gang, so that they could get as full a picture of their operation as possible.

He also thought it was sensible for Emma to stay out of sight in my flat, and she made no objection.

Neither did I.

Chapter 11

I hadn't expected to have some one-to-one time with Emma quite so quickly, and in these unusual circumstances I didn't want to seem to be taking advantage.

Sure, I liked her. I liked her very much now that I knew she was not involved in some intricate plot against Mobilicity, and not stringing me along for some devious purpose; but I had only known her for a couple of days, and I was anxious not to seem to be rushing things.

We spent a companionable afternoon chatting. Uncle Jim had advised Emma not to go out under any circumstances – if they knew she was free it would upset the whole operation – so it was my pleasure to keep her company.

I apologised for having doubted her, even up to the point when I found her tied up in the shed. She confessed to me that she wondered which side I was on, and whether I was part of the laundering scam. She apologised for invading my bedroom, but insisted that she had no idea I was there, and was frightened out of her life when I jumped her. She also forgave me for having doubted her – she could quite see that from my point of view her actions and her story must have seemed totally bizarre. Having forgiven each other for the doubts we had each entertained, we changed the subject.

So, we talked about more usual things. I discovered that she had many friends locally, but no particular boyfriend at the moment. She commented that she had to put in a lot of time getting started in accountancy, and this did not leave much scope for serious socialising since she had to study for her exams as well as doing a day's work. She said she was on a graduate conversion course, which meant that she learned the business as a sort of apprentice, at first shadowing her qualified colleagues, and then gradually being allowed to take on accounts by herself as she gained experience. She also had to study in her own time, and take some pretty demanding exams at regular intervals. She was determined to get these exams at first time of asking, and not mess about for years as some people seemed to. She also added with brutal honesty, "Serious boyfriends can take lots of time which I don't have at the moment."

"However," she continued archly, "with any luck, it shouldn't be long before I qualify, and then it will be a different matter."

I felt encouraged by this, and said so.

"I'm in much the same boat," I confided. "Starting on a new career takes a lot of extra time, though the effort is worth it in the end. But I don't want to end up a workaholic like James – I don't think his family ever see him for more than about five hours a week, and that is mostly for meals at the weekend. He's brilliant, of course, but – well, I think there's more to life than the daily grind."

"You seem to have made an impressive start as far as he is concerned – James' blue-eyed boy, except that you have brown eyes."

I don't know why I should have felt pleased that she had noticed, but I was.

"I think I have been very lucky. I'm doing what I am interested in; it is what I studied at college, and it is not all that number of graduates who have the opportunity to use their degree as a basis for a career. What did you read?"

"You won't even begin to guess."

"What, then? Maths? Economics?" She shook her head.

"Psychology?" I hazarded.

"No," she said, amused, "Classics."

"Classics?"

"Yes, it sounds ridiculous, doesn't it? I chose to read classics because I wanted to. I actually enjoyed it; but, to be brutally frank, I was able to learn Latin at school and thought that it would be easier to get into a decent university course because most of their classics departments are only too pleased to welcome any student because there are so few about. I had to learn some Greek, though. That was a bit of a struggle."

"I bet it was. But how do you get to do accountancy after graduating?"

"Well, it seems that accountancy firms prefer to look at the person rather than what degree they have got. Everyone has do the separate accountancy exams anyway, so provided you have a reasonably logical mind and are literate and numerate, and they think you will get on with people, they train you in their own way. You'd be surprised how many different degrees can be found amongst accountants. I think it's a good thing."

"It's a shame you can't use your classics though," I persisted.

"Well, there aren't many careers in translating Horace odes or declaiming Virgil in public, but it still has its uses."

"Such as?"

"Spelling, for a start; and crosswords. Lately, it has been invaluable in recognising the Latin spells and incantations in the Harry Potter books, and feeling smug that I know what they mean. Really useful things like that."

I was glad she had a sense of humour.

"However," she continued, "I do get to meet a great variety of people, and they have a wide range of problems. Many people don't understand about money, and it can be very satisfying showing them ways of handling their financial problems. Of course there are technical things to know, like the tax laws, but as often as not it comes down to people. I like that."

She asked me about my brief time at Mobilicity.

"Well, I'm fortunate enough to have fallen on my feet and found at first time of asking a job that really suits me. James has got some great concepts, but he's useless at efficient production. It's the same with many creative people. You heard what he said about the Stores?"

"Yes, he gave you a lot of credit for sorting it out."

"I know, but he didn't tell the half of it. It was absolute chaos. The first time I went in there I counted twenty-five axle sets for our electric wheelchair. They were just sitting there, taking up space, doing nothing. I asked how long this stock would keep us supplied. Nobody knew. I asked how many chairs were being made, and was told 'quite a lot'. I then asked how many were on the order books, and heard that there were 'some'. I asked how goods were ordered, and learnt that as soon as someone saw something was running out, they ordered a whole lot more. 'How many more?' I asked, and was told 'it depended'. 'What does it depend on?' I asked. 'Well - on how many we think we'll need', they said. 'How do you know how many you will need?' I enquired.

'Don't ask me – if you're so bloody clever, work it out for yourself', I was told."

"This, of course, was Gary. It also transpired that there was no control on whoever took what out. If someone dropped, say, an axle casing, and it broke, they simply went and took another one. How are you supposed to keep track of anything like that?"

"Sorry. I'm going on."

I know my own enthusiasms are not always shared by others, especially girls, and I decided it was more than time to shut up; but I was astonished to find that Emma seemed genuinely interested.

"No, really, I like to hear about how other people operate and if you weren't keen on what you are doing, you wouldn't do it half as well. I can quite see why James appointed you; and I have also seen what effect you have had on the company in less than two years. I think you ought to be very proud of yourself. I would be."

I was pleasantly flattered.

"I suppose," I said after a pause, "that our jobs have something in common. We both need to have some formal qualifications, but as often as not it comes down to using what we know to help sort other people out. It's all about people rather than principles, isn't it? I'd never thought of it like that before."

Emma wholeheartedly agreed, and we finished up confirming the strong compatibility between production engineering and accountancy. It was all very satisfactory.

Unlike this morning, time flew by, and it began to get dark.

Emma said, "I think the least I can do in return for your hospitality is to cook some supper. What have you got?"

"Well, I was going to have a stir-fry. I've got some chicken bits and the onions and veg and some bean sprouts. I have also got some coconut milk and some chillies, because I wondered about trying some Thai recipes, though I believe they are a bit hot. What do you think?"

"I'm amazed," said Emma, and she looked it. "I thought bachelors all lived on baked beans, sausages and oven chips washed down by Boddingtons. I'm impressed."

"I can manage the Boddingtons if I have to, but in the fridge there's a bottle of Pouilly-Vinzelles which I was going to try."

I knew I was showing off. I'm not a wine buff, but the previous autumn I had a holiday in Burgundy. I enjoyed the Macon wines, and brought back some Pouilly-Vinzelles because it sounded great, and cost a lot less than the more famous Pouilly-Fuisse.

She answered in kind. "But of course. I never drink anything else." We both grinned.

"You seem to do yourself very well," she said with approval. "And yes, I can just about manage a stir-fry. Do you have a wok?"

"Fortunately, I do. My elder sister Liz gave me one last Christmas in one of her periodic attempts to 'civilise' me."

"She seems to have succeeded," she said, obviously approving of the stratagems of elder sisters.

I produced the wok with a flourish, and she donned an apron because she still had only her blue professional outfit to wear and wanted to keep the spats off. I rummaged round for the necessary ingredients; and having decided on not too hot a meal - we omitted the green Thai curry paste and most of the chillies.

She also thought about organising a dessert, which I had to admit I had not allowed for.

Emma chopped up the chicken and the vegetables with the easy competence of a practised cook, and before long we were sitting down to an excellent Thai stir-fry *a la* Emma.

"That was great," I said pouring out the last of the wine. "We should do this more often."

"You haven't had pudding yet," she said. "You'd better withhold judgement."

Pudding was simple, but just the sort of thing I like, especially considering she had to make do with whatever I happened to have. It consisted of banana, halved and quartered, with two scoops of dairy ice-cream, all topped with dark chocolate which she had melted in the microwave, and garnished with chopped almonds.

I did not speak until we were finishing.

"As I was saying, that was great. We should do this *much* more often."

She glowed.

"Thank you, kind sir," she said. "I might very well take you up on that. But the whole effect might have been ruined if you had not had a carton of Winstone's Dairy in the freezer."

"I'm never without it," I replied, with a fair degree of accuracy. "I'm sorry it wasn't rum and raisin."

"Wouldn't have been the same at all," she said mock-sniffily. "It doesn't go with banana."

We washed up the things by hand. I don't have a dishwasher – well, it's not worth it just for one – and in any case it is much more companionable to be engaged in some routine chore while just enjoying each other's company. We finished putting things away, and I decided to make a cup of real coffee, as it was a special occasion.

Well, it had somehow become a special occasion. I knew that our proximity was artificial, but that simply didn't seem to matter. I had begun to realise that I was getting absolutely serious about Emma. There was no point in trying to rationalise what I felt. I just knew that we seemed so comfortable together. I liked the way she looked, the way she talked, the way she could listen as well as say things worth listening to; I liked the way she laughed, I enjoyed her obvious intelligence, I appreciated her concern for others. Above all, I felt that we both had a strong rapport, and could each think in the way the other thought almost instinctively. I even thought she might have similar feelings for me.

We sat together on the sofa, and when our coffee cups were finally drained she snuggled down into the cushions and rested her head on my shoulder.

I had my Bix Beiderbecke original tracks playing softly in the background.

"I like classical jazz," she said simply "and I've really enjoyed today."

I put an arm round her shoulders.

"So have I. I wouldn't mind it going on for a lot longer."

There was a pause.

"About tomorrow," she said. "You won't be in any danger will you?"

"I shouldn't think so. Your Uncle Jim seems to have everything sorted out, and I don't see what could go wrong. Why do you ask?"

"Well – I just don't want anything to happen to you. I think you have done enough already."

"For goodness sake, I have only got to go to a restaurant and leave a disc there. Where's the problem?"

"I don't know. It's just that the disc is so important, and if this Russell whatever-he-is realises he is being conned he could do anything. Think what he had in mind for my fingers."

"I know. It made me feel sick just thinking about it. But the whole point is to get him arrested with the disc, and he'll only come if he thinks I will give it to him; otherwise he'll just disappear. This is the only way to fix him and his whole operation. Also, Steve might have another chance in life. There's an awful lot depending on this. I understand how you feel, Emma, but I really don't think there is a serious risk. Even if they did realise something was wrong, Uncle Jim's boys will be on hand to prevent anything awful happening to me. Won't they?"

She sort of agreed, and we let the matter drop. I appreciated the fact that she was obviously concerned for my well-being, but I couldn't help feeling that she was being a touch over-anxious.

I thought about it, but couldn't see what could possibly go wrong.

We spent the rest of the evening listening to music, companionably snuggled up on the sofa.

I had been considering for quite a while what would happen at the end of the evening. Last night, while I was on the sofa, Emma had slept in my bed, and Linus was in the spare room.

I had no doubt in my own mind what I would like to do, and that was to join Emma in my bed, but I had a horrible feeling that to move things along too quickly could lead to the end of a beautiful relationship. She might feel that I had taken her too much for granted in our enforced closeness, and that was the last thing I wanted.

Therefore, when we decided to turn in, I indicated that I would occupy the spare room, and she could sleep in my room again. Since she had no clothes other than what she stood up in, I had lent her a short-sleeved cotton leisure shirt. I suggested that she might like to use the bathroom first.

She looked at me for a moment, seemed to understand the situation, kissed me good-night and went to change, while I waited in the spare room. It was not long before she was out of the bathroom, and the door shut quietly behind her.

I paused, wondering if I was doing the right thing. Anyhow, I had made my decision, so I showered and did my teeth and returned to the spare room.

I lay there for some time, thinking about the rapidly changing events of the last couple of days, about drugs, about Russell Deverell – but most particularly about Emma.

I thought that of the various girlfriends I had known, I had never felt like this about any of them. I couldn't believe that I had really only known her for less than three days, and yet I felt I knew more about her than I had known about any of the others in months. I knew with absolute certainty that this was the girl I wanted to spend the rest of my life with. All the siren voices were telling me that 'it was much too early to make such an important decision'. I listened briefly – and then told them to get lost. When they changed tack, and warned that she might not feel the same, I countered by saying I'd bet they were wrong, and that I was willing to risk it. Whatever happened, I was going to go on seeing her after this was all over, and my every instinct told me that she would want us to continue.

Secure in these certainties, I was just about to doze off when I was aware of my door opening.

It was Emma, resplendent in my magenta shirt. She looked stunning.

"Oliver?"

"Yes?"

"I don't quite know how to put this. I know you don't want to be seen to be pushy, and I appreciate that. But – can I stay with you tonight?"

"Of course." I only just avoided adding, 'Please.'

She seemed to need to explain herself.

"It was what happened yesterday. It shook me up more than I realised. Every creak of the door, or car passing by, and I get the frights. I know it's silly. Do you mind?"

By way of answer, I sat up and pulled the duvet well off. She got in, and immediately we were in each other's arms.

"This is the second time in three days you have invaded my sleeping quarters," I said, kissing her nose.

"I know," she said, running her fingers down my spine.

"Might it happen again?" I asked anxiously, undoing the magenta shirt.

"Sure to," she murmured, as we uninhibitedly embraced. "Quite often, I hope."

Chapter 12

I felt ready for anything when I woke up. It was still early, and Emma snoozed on while I made a cup of tea and took it to her. The offer of it seemed to wake her up.

"Oooh, room service as well," she purred. "I think I might come here again."

"Reservations always available," I said, and kissed her, narrowly avoiding spilling her tea all over the duvet.

We idly got ourselves up and made a simple breakfast. We didn't say a lot, but preferred to rejoice in each other's presence and the remembrance of last night. We had a lot to remember.

Gradually, though, the thought of the venture to come returned to the uppermost part of our thoughts, and we awaited the arrival of Uncle Jim with increasing impatience. He arrived soon after ten, and briefed us fully on what had happened at his end.

"The disc was absolutely first class. You could tell that it had been compiled by an accountant, everything was there and in order and cross referenced. We have the complete run-down on the whole operation."

"Were you able to take a copy, or will we have to give back the only one?" asked Emma, her professional curiosity getting the better of her.

"What do you think?" said Uncle Jim smugly. "Of course we were able to copy it in *toto*. There's not much our lads can't copy if they put their Machiavellian minds to it. Yes, we've got it all – but of course, our friend Russell D can't know this. He almost certainly thinks this is the only one in existence."

"Then he will be very anxious to get it, won't he?" asked Emma thoughtfully.

"Anxious? He'll be desperate," replied her uncle. "That's what I'm counting on. What's more, it is so important, that he will almost certainly come to collect it himself. As soon as he has it in his hands, we can move in and arrest him. That really is the only way we can connect him to the racket, apart from demanding his signature from the bank, and that may not be easy – you know what banks are like."

"What happens if he discovers that we have rescued Emma and Linus?" I wanted to know. "Surely he will then be on his guard. What happens if he doesn't turn up?"

"Yes, that might be a problem," said Uncle Jim. "However, you said that he and his sidekick would not phone each other, and I think it unlikely that they would do so until the agreed exchange has been made. I am quite sure he would have intended to keep his word. All he is really concerned with is getting the disc back, and the only alternative to releasing Emma would be to murder her. I certainly don't think he would want to be involved in murder. Mutilation perhaps, yes. But murder, I don't think so."

I felt appalled that he could so casually consider even the possibility of Emma being killed in cold blood. I suppose he was used to these scenarios, but I had never realised it might have applied to Emma. I was thinking how glad I was that we had rescued her when another thought struck me.

"But what would he have done with Linus, knowing him to be a traitor as far as he was concerned?" I persisted.

"Interesting point," he replied. "I discussed this with Linus, and he seemed to think Russell would pressure him into signing whatever was necessary, and then let him go. The money in the account would then be somewhere else where Linus had no access, and without the disc Linus would, he imagined, have no proof that would stand up in court. It would also be very difficult for Linus not to appear as a willing part of the racket – or so Russell would think. Remember, Russell didn't know that a second copy of Linus' letter of intent was lodged safely at the bank.

"No. I feel sure that our friend Russell D thinks everything will be fine providing he can get the disc back. That will be his one and only priority, and I am betting on him coming in person to collect it."

"You've got this famous disc with you, I assume," I said.

"Certainly," said Uncle Jim, producing it. "and, for that matter, I've got a spare Waitrose bag just in case you didn't have one."

I took the disc and examined it.

"It's hard to imagine that such a harmless-looking thing can be the cause of so much trouble," I commented.

"You have to see what a catalogue of human misery it represents," replied Uncle Jim. "That simple bit of plastic represents the broken lives of a great many people."

"Yes," said Emma. "But it also represents a huge fortune which desperate men will not want to give up easily. I don't like to think of exposing Oliver to unnecessary danger."

Her uncle looked at her, and then at me, and seemed to come to a rapid conclusion. I didn't think we had been as obvious as that, but he was a shrewd man.

"I shouldn't dream of it," he said thoughtfully. "Remember that my men will be on hand, three inside and two outside the building covering the entrance. They will be armed, but I think it highly unlikely that arms will be necessary. I have every reason to believe that our friend will want to get his disc back with as little fuss as possible. Drawing attention to himself will be the last thing he'll want to do.

"So, just to remind ourselves of the order of events, my men will be in and out of the bar area from opening time, about twelve o'clock. Oliver will come in at just after half-past, and ask for the table booked in his name. We've checked where this will be so our men will know, but it will look more natural if Oliver gets the bar staff to tell him where it is. He will order a drink and something quick to prepare and eat – a ploughman's or some such – and sit down at the table with the bag, which he will casually put down on the deep sill of the window by the table.

"He will eat his meal quite slowly, and not leave until just after ten past one. We don't want anyone trying to occupy the table, even if it is booked. It might be a good idea to take a Sunday paper, and be reading that. Anyway, he needs to look entirely at ease and natural – don't on any account keep looking around and appearing to identify people. That might just make them nervous.

"When the time comes, Oliver, wander up to the counter leaving the bag with the disc by the window. It is pretty well obscured from sight. Pay your bill, and then leave by the main entrance. Remember, you are supposed to be returning to your flat to get the final instructions for releasing Emma."

"Shall I go back to the flat?" I wanted to know.

"You can if you want to, but you might just as well stay out of sight outside with our men and see the fun. I'll be in the reception area up the stairs from the main entrance. It should only take a minute or two. He will sit down and check the bag and its contents because he will need to be sure he has the right disc. As soon as he does this, and his prints are all over it, we will arrest him."

I had to admit that this all seemed very unproblematic and even Emma seemed less anxious than before.

"What shall I be doing while all this is happening?" she wanted to know.

"Well, you can come along with me, if you like," said her uncle. "I shall have Linus with me to identify the person who collects. If you and he are out of sight until our friend has entered the building there should be no problem. Of course, you mustn't be seen by him beforehand – that would give the whole game away."

"I hope I'm not entirely stupid," she retorted with some vigour. "But yes, I would like to be there. I want to see him caught and I also want to see that nothing awful happens to Oliver."

I don't think she quite meant to speak as decidedly as that, and she reddened; but her uncle had more sense than to notice.

I liked Uncle Jim even more.

The plans being settled, we all had a cup of coffee and chatted for a few minutes. Then Emma went with her Uncle, saying that we should all meet up for a celebratory drink after the arrest had been made. The two of us did not make a fond farewell with Uncle Jim there, but I managed to give her hand a surreptitious squeeze before they left.

It was by now twenty to twelve, so I had a little over half an hour to kill before I set out on what I hoped would be the last part of this whole astonishing affair.

Three days ago, everything had been as normal, a routine day at the office. I could never have imagined that I would have been beaten up, been presented with a kidnapping, become aware of a major drugs racket being channelled through my own firm, effected a rescue, discovered new allies, and was now on course to have a master criminal arrested.

I was also very much aware of how much I wanted to give Steve the chance of recovering from his addiction. Naturally, I knew that various student acquaintances had experimented with drugs, but it was only when I had come face to face with Steve, and had heard his story from Gary, that I fully realised the appallingly destructive effects drug addiction can have on people. It was such a waste of an intelligent young life. When I thought of what Linus had said about his father, it dawned on me that drug addiction was not the sole prerogative of inexperienced youth, but in different circumstances it could affect anyone of any age.

In addition, I felt somehow honoured that it had by chance fallen to me to bring to justice the people who were promoting all this human misery. I had no idea who Russell Deverell was, but what from what I had personally experienced of his character, and from what Linus had been able to tell me, he was one of the most dangerous and amoral criminals around, trading vulnerable human weakness for huge personal profit. I felt that it would not only be a duty but also a pleasure to put him behind bars.

But of all the changes that had taken place in these three days, the best and most important was the entry into my life of Emma.

After she had come in to me the night before, all my most optimistic hopes and speculations had been confirmed, and all my fears put aside. She told me how comfortable she felt we were together, and how easy it was to confide in each other. She said that although she had not been looking to settle down just yet, that must have been because she had not found anyone she wanted to settle down with – until she found me.

Her thoughts couldn't have matched my own more exactly, and the previous night we had found that we were compatible in a number of other ways, too. She had wondered whether the jumpiness, which had persuaded her to come to me for comfort, had been a sufficient excuse for her behaviour, and I assured her that jumpiness would be my favourite character trait from now on. She also felt, with hindsight, that I might have been unnecessarily gentlemanly in arranging separate rooms; and I assured her that gentlemen can sometimes be exceedingly stupid – and promised that it wouldn't happen again.

I broke into my happy reverie, and prepared to leave on what should be the last stage of our plan. I collected the Waitrose bag and its precious contents, put the answer-phone on in case anyone should ring, and had a final look round to check that I had everything I needed – money, mobile, bag.

I briefly considered Emma's apprehension about the whole operation. Was there a real risk? I accepted that Russell would be desperate to get the disc back, even though he could have no idea that it had been copied by the police and was even now building a formidable case against the gang. I also hoped that he had not discovered our successful rescue operation, because he would know that his position would be desperate if we had both Emma and Linus out of his control. He might do anything.

On the other hand, even if he had found out, he surely wouldn't risk an attempt to abduct me from Egypt Mill. We would obviously have set a trap, though he couldn't know whether the police were involved since his threat to proclaim Linus as part of the gang might have discouraged official involvement. Even so, if he realised we now had all his hostages out of harm's way, I would only keep the appointment in order to entrap him.

No. I reckoned that, if he came, it would be because he thought the original arrangements stood, and it would offer him the best chance of getting his disc back. If he was suspicious, he would pull out and try something else. I thought it highly unlikely that he would try any rough stuff in the bar; and if he did, then Uncle Jim's men were there to sort it out. I was pleased that Emma had shown concern for my safety – bless her! – but I felt absolutely certain that going to the rendezvous was virtually risk-free.

I picked up my jacket and left the flat on a high, delighted with the prospect of a future with Emma, and the chance of doing something to help put Russell Deverell behind the bars as he so richly deserved.

I had the wit to observe that everything was normal up and down the road, and checked the van briefly before strapping myself in and setting off for the Egypt Mill, my lunch, and a date with destiny.

It was twenty past twelve.

Chapter 13

The Egypt Mill at Nailsworth was originally one of the many textile mills set in the valleys converging on Stroud. There is a constant supply of water from the rivulets draining into the valley bottoms to supply the power for the water wheels, which drove the machines of the nineteenth and early twentieth century cotton and wool industries.

Nobody quite knows how this particular mill got its name. I was interested enough to enquire when I had been there once before and someone suggested it was because Egyptian cotton was used in the fabric produced at one time. However, when the cloth industry declined and the mill closed its doors as a factory for the last time, the name was retained, together with the machinery and the vast millpond which had been dammed to provide the water necessary to drive its two huge water wheels. The whole site had been taken over and turned into a restaurant and events complex. The lower floor was retained as a bar and pub food outlet.

The impressive water wheels were still in their original position, completely visible from the bar but carefully enclosed by glass partitions to conform to health and safety standards. Much additional evidence of the building's industrial past had been carefully preserved and even enhanced to emphasise the general theme, and everything projected an overall impression of unusual authenticity.

It was twenty-five to one when I parked my van in the huge parking area and crossed over the bridge, which led to the mill itself.

Clutching a Sunday paper stuffed into my Waitrose bag, I descended the stone steps and strolled into the bar area. Opposite the main entrance was a doorway leading to a few alfresco tables at the edge of the impressive millpond, which encompassed the entire area.

The bar was not yet crowded. A few of the tables were occupied with casual drinkers, and there were half a dozen men leaning up against the bar chatting about this and that. A perfectly normal Sunday lunchtime scene.

I gained the barman's attention.

"I believe there is a table reserved for me – name of Howsen."

He flicked through his diary.

"Yes," he said. "It's rather strange, because the same table has been reserved for one fifteen. I hope you don't mind hurrying. Whoever booked it said it would be all right."

I felt I needed to give some explanation.

"No, that's OK. My friend and I are looking after his wife who has flu and we don't want to leave her alone. She's feeling awful, so we thought we would come out separately, and wanted to make sure there would be a table later on when it gets crowded."

"Oh, right." This explanation seemed to satisfy him. "There seems to be a lot of flu about," he added in the conversation-continuing manner of all barmen. When it became clear that I had no wish to stand there chatting about fictitious flu symptoms, he pointed to a table on the far side of the bar.

"Over there. You shouldn't be disturbed."

I ordered Stilton ploughman's lunch and a pint of Old Spot, and went where he directed me.

My table was up the steps, which led to the millpond opposite the bar. It was next to a small window with a deep ledge. Russell had chosen well; I could place my bag there quite naturally, and it would be easy to forget it when I left. It would also be out of sight to anyone not actually concerned with my table.

I casually placed my bag on the sill, took out the paper, and took a long swig of my beer. I thought I would take a brief look at the place before my ploughman's arrived.

It was quite a large bar area, with another room situated on the far side behind the bar. At one end, the smaller of the two water wheels revolved lazily in its glass compartment, while up my end the larger wheel stood determinedly static. It was a substantial structure and conveyed a feeling of awesome power despite its lack of movement. This impression was heightened by the sound and sight of water gushing from the millpond into the sluice under the massive paddles. The temptation to open the sluice gate just a little and set the whole thing in motion was almost too much for my engineering instincts to resist.

The rest of the space was occupied with a dozen or so tables and various theme-items, which were designed to remind patrons of the building's industrial past. It resembled a room in an industrial folk museum.

I cast a surreptitious eye over the other customers, trying to guess which were Uncle Jim's men and which might be Russell's. Annoyingly, everyone seemed entirely normal. None of them looked anxious or out of place. There were two couples chatting by themselves, and one or two lone males presumably waiting to be joined by others, and two men in their twenties chatted at the bar. Not one seemed to be taking the slightest interest in me, and all of them appeared to be ordinary citizens enjoying a Sunday drink.

My attempt to distinguish friend or foe was a complete failure.

My ploughman's came, and I ate it slowly, determinedly engaged in my paper. The minutes ticked by, and gradually the bar began to fill up. I could quite see why it was necessary for my particular table to be reserved because by one o'clock all the other tables were occupied.

Nobody took the slightest notice of me.

At just after ten past one, I tucked my paper under my arm, moved the 'reserved' sign into a clearly prominent position, and made my way to the bar to pay my bill. I left the bag with the disc in it neatly folded on the window sill, out of sight from the lower part of the bar area.

I walked as naturally as I could out and up the steps and was about to cross the bridge when I was intercepted by Uncle Jim.

"Oliver, come up here."

I went up to the next floor where there was a sort of reception room where he and a couple of his men were seated. So were Emma and Linus.

"We are controlling things from here," Uncle Jim explained. "So far everything has gone to plan. You did very well."

"How can you say that?" I enquired, moving over to be next to Emma. "You weren't there."

Uncle Jim chuckled.

"One of my men has a two-way radio discreetly hidden about his person. Did you happen to notice a young lad at the far end who was apparently listening to his personal stereo while waiting for his oppo to turn up?"

I had to confess I hadn't.

"Well, while he is apparently mouthing the words of his choice of hit song, he's actually giving us a minute by minute account of what's happening."

He turned to one of his men with earphones.

"What's new, Ian?" he asked.

Ian relayed the information as he got it.

"Possible suspect has entered the bar area, and is making enquiries. Yes, he is being directed to the reserved table. He is taking a glass of red wine with him and has gone there to wait for his order. He is sitting down. He has a Sunday paper and is reading it. So far he has shown no interest in the disc."

There was a pause.

"Playing it casual," commented Ian.

"Wouldn't you?" said Uncle Jim. "The last thing he wants to do is to draw attention to himself. If he suspected a trap, he would want to play the innocent. He would advertise his guilt by grabbing the disc and scarpering."

Emma whispered 'Well done' in my ear, and gave my hand a squeeze. I put my arm round her shoulder. "Sorry I sounded so concerned about it. I've never been involved in anything like this before, and I … well…" She paused. "Anyway, you were right – there was no problem. But I'm glad it's all over."

"We'll discuss it later," I whispered back, giving her shoulder an encouraging hug.

Ian continued his report.

"Suspect has his meal, lasagne by the look of it. He has still not opened the bag, but is concentrating on his paper. Wait a minute – he has noticed the bag. No, he has gone back to reading."

There was a pause, which seemed endless. We waited in silence.

"He's finished his meal. Yes, he's pretended to notice the bag. He's opening it. He is now taking out the disc – and examining it behind his paper. He's giving it a long hard look. He seems satisfied."

There was a short pause.

"Suspect is now taking out his mobile. He's looking slowly round the room, but can't see anything amiss.

"He's dialling a number, and talking. He is speaking low, not like the usual blather everyone has to listen to.

"He's stopped. He's having another look round, as though he can't believe it. No; he seems satisfied. He's signed off, and is putting the phone away."

"He's probably phoning you," said Uncle Jim. "Telling you where you can find Emma. As soon as he gets up, we'll arrest him. Very neat and tidy, if I may say so."

Ian's line crackled.

"Bloody hell."

There was a shocked reaction from all of us.

Ian spoke urgently.

"One of our idiots failed to turn off his radio, and at the crucial moment there was a police message and the target has got suspicious. He's dropped the disc on the table – he's panicking – he's looking round nervously – he's got up. Now he's making a beeline for the doors out to the millpond."

I turned to Uncle Jim.

"I'm going down. If he's making a run for it, I want to make sure we have the disc," and with that I legged it down the two flights of steps and into the bar. I rushed straight over to the table I had vacated, and there, lying innocently on the cloth, was the disc. I quickly stuffed it into my pocket, and looked round to see what had happened to Russell.

Two of Uncle Jim's men were already at the doorway, and did not seem surprised when I joined them. Russell was frantically looking for a way out of the complex, but found himself surrounded by water

Uncle Jim's men grinned.

"He can't get away," one of them said. "He is marooned. It's a pity he hasn't got the disc actually on him – we would have preferred that – but we can pick him up as we wish."

Unfortunately, he had underestimated the ingenuity of their quarry.

The fugitive jumped up on the side housing-block for the sluice of the large wheel, and swung himself down so that he was immediately in front of the wheel itself. Slowly, very slowly, he stood on the heavy damp board on the top of the sluice itself, and side-footed his way to the other side with astonishing agility. Then he managed to swing himself nimbly on to the housing block on the far side, and took stock.

There was a look of desperation on his face. His only route to escape to his car was across the rivulet, which flowed out of the millpond, and this consisted of a deeply muddied millpond on one side, and a steep, rocky drop on the other. The only thing spanning this area was a deep u-shaped structure of coping stone set edge-up, which marked the boundary of the pond and the descent of the river.

It seemed impossible to cross, but our quarry saw a way to do it. He again side-footed his way across the wet surface, and even though he had no hand-holds to help him as he had in front of the wheel, he managed to keep his balance with astonishing skill. I had to admire his effort as slowly, but with increasing confidence, he worked his way round the first section of the stone coping, recovered after appearing to slip during the course of the second section, and then manoeuvred his feet to negotiate the last section of the u-bend.

Suddenly, he lost his footing on the slimy stone edging, and despite a desperate flailing of arms he found it impossible to maintain any sort of equilibrium. Hopelessly off balance, he fell into the rock-strewn riverbed some feet below where he remained motionless, immersed in a cascade of water.

His mobile phone started to ring insistently.

Two of Uncle Jim's men went across the bridge, and clambered down to where the prostrate body lay. They pulled him out and examined him briefly.

"Call an ambulance. Amongst other things, he has a depressed fracture of the skull. It's quite likely he won't make it."

While we waited for the ambulance to arrive, we managed to acquire a stretcher from Egypt Mill and carried him up to the reception room. Uncle Jim made some hurried arrangements for one of his team to accompany the injured man to hospital and stand guard in case he should awake.

Emma came over to me and whispered that she was glad I was all right, and at least that was now all over.

Linus had been sitting some way away while all this was going on, and now he came over to where we were all congregated.

He looked at our captive. He spent several moments earnestly surveying the swollen and blood-streaked face that presented itself to his gaze.

"Oh," he said.

Uncle Jim gave him a quick glance.

"What's the matter?"

Linus paused.

"Well," he said, "I know he has been a little disfigured by his fall, but I'm afraid I have some bad news. Whoever this is, it is not Russell Deverell."

There was a stunned silence.

"Not Russell?" asked Uncle Jim. "You're absolutely sure?"

"No question about it, I'm afraid. Russell has a dimpled chin and black hair. As you can see, this man is almost blond, and if anything has a receding chin. I've no idea who he is, but he is definitely not Russell."

"Bugger," said Uncle Jim.

Chapter 14

We all felt a mixture of emotions when we realised that Russell Deverell was still at large.

Why had he sent some junior member of his gang, if the disc was so important? Could it be that he had found out about us rescuing Emma, and was not risking a possible trap?

Perhaps he thought the whole thing was so simple that it didn't need his personal supervision. If that was the case, he'd soon find out that we had not handed the disc over – and then what would he do?

"He's got to try to get it back," Uncle Jim commented gloomily. "He can't possibly allow that disc to fall into our hands, especially now that he knows that we set a trap for him."

"He won't know that the police are involved, though," I put in hopefully. "The lad he sent to get it panicked before he could let Russell know of the police presence. It could just have been us trying to do a deal with him, or something. After all, that's what Gary would have done with the disc."

Uncle Jim considered for a moment.

"It's possible, but I don't think he will take the risk. He can't. He's got to have that disc, and he has got to have Linus as the other signatory necessary to retrieve his money. So, Linus, you will stay with us until we have him. Sorry, but he will certainly try to snatch you as soon as he realises that you and Emma have been freed.

"That leaves the disc. He'll know that we've got it, Oliver, because no doubt his man told him about it when he made that phone-call; he can't have thought how to get it back. There hasn't been time. He'll soon find out that he has lost his hostages, even if he doesn't know already. That'll put him in something of a fix, but he'll have to do something, and do it quickly."

"He might simply try to buy it back," I suggested. "He can't realise that we have read it – as far as he knows, the disc cannot be read," I suggested.

"Again, it's possible," Uncle Jim replied. "The trouble is we just don't know how much he is aware of the situation. If he doesn't yet know about the rescue of Linus and Emma, he'll find out – it's the first thing he will check on. We must keep Emma as well as Linus well out of harm's way. He has to have Linus, and might try to take Emma as a hostage again if he gets the chance."

We brooded on the difficulties of the situation, not knowing what to do, but somehow aware that there was a need for urgent action. We guessed we had the advantage of surprise at the moment, but suspected that Russell would be quick to regroup once he found out how the land lay. I suddenly woke up.

"Of course! I am supposed to be getting a phone call from him at my flat. There is no reason to suppose he will not try to contact me in the way we agreed. I'll nip back home and see if there's a message, and we can take it from there."

"I'll come with you," said Emma.

"Oh no you won't," said Uncle Jim decisively. "You're staying with us. You've got your mobile, Oliver? OK, then, go now see if there is any message. Give us a quick call if there is one, and, message or not, come straight back. We'll finish clearing up here, and then decide what we do next."

This seemed a sensible enough suggestion and at least I felt I was doing something positive, rather than sitting around wondering. It took less than ten minutes to reach my flat, and I leapt straight out and through my front door.

I went directly to the phone, and was disappointed to find that there were no calls. I dialled 1471 and found the last call was well before I had left this morning.

I felt a sudden deflation of spirit. I wondered how long I should wait before returning empty-handed – after all, Russell had not given a time for calling – he just said he would ring as soon as the disc had been checked. It couldn't have taken long, if he had got it.

Then again, he might not know what had happened to his man, and simply be waiting for him to appear, though I couldn't imagine him not having some of his men around observing what went on. It was too important for him to leave things to chance.

Suddenly, the phone rang.

I grabbed it frantically.

"Congratulations! Someone in your household has won a major award in our recent competition…"

"Oh, shut up!" I shouted in more than usual annoyance and slammed the phone down.

I waited another ten minutes in impatient silence. Then I took out my mobile and phoned Emma.

"Hello," she said. "Any news?"

"Absolutely nothing, not a sausage. Can I have a word with Uncle Jim?"

She handed over to him.

"I'm afraid there is nothing at all. There have been no calls since I left, apart from a prat probably trying to get me to buy time-share."

"You're sure that was genuine? It wasn't someone just wishing to make sure you are at home?"

I had considered that possibility.

"No, I'm sure it wasn't. It was a recorded message. There would be no need to go through that rigmarole if they just wanted to check I was at home."

"Still," said Uncle Jim thoughtfully, "I think you should come straight back. I'll see you in about ten minutes."

I set the burglar alarm and opened the door. I checked carefully up and down the street, turning over in my mind what we could do next. Thus pre-occupied, I got into the van, reversed out, and set off towards Nailsworth.

I could only have been driving for two or three minutes when I felt something hard and cold against the back of my neck.

A familiar voice spoke gently in my ear.

"Yes, this is a gun, and I may have to use it if you do not do exactly as I tell you."

Russell Deverell. It had to be. I recognised instantly the voice of the man who mugged me at the start of all this.

"I shall move the gun lower, so that it will not be so obvious to the world in general," he continued conversationally. "But don't be misled into thinking it is not pointing straight at your stomach. Being shot in the stomach is a very painful death, they tell me. Follow my directions, and no harm will come to you. Turn left here."

I glanced in my rear view mirror and saw my assailant for the first time. He gave the impression of being immaculately clad in a blazer and cavalry twill way. He was in his thirties, and as Linus had said, he had dark hair and his healthily tanned features were set off by a dimpled chin. He looked impeccably respectable.

"Left again up here and then keep straight on."

I did as I was told. I had no option, really.

"You know," he continued casually, "You have only yourself to blame. I warned you about leaving your vehicle unlocked. You really ought to have listened."

The annoying thing was that he was right – he had and I ought. All he'd needed to do was to get in the back of the van and crouch down behind the seat and, my mind on other things, I fell for it hook line and sinker. I had been a complete idiot.

I was being directed up the hill towards Rodborough Common, and I drove slowly to give myself a bit of time to think.

I rapidly tried to assess my captor.

It was no good getting in a strop about my position, whatever I might feel about him. He obviously liked to play the part of laid-back gentleman operator who just happened to work outside the law. He would probably be able to justify his trade by arguing that he was merely meeting a demand; or that people had the right to choose how they lived their lives or spent their money. But despite the outward pose of civility, I felt that behind the *façade* was a ruthless streak which would brook no opposition, and I remembered Linus' description of him - 'an absolute bastard'. Linus did not use that sort of language without reason.

I formed the strong impression that Russell was not so much immoral as amoral – he simply did not see that there was anything wrong in what he did for a living, or the means he used to achieve his ends; and had the enviable knack of being able to shut his eyes to any of the resulting evil.

I decided I would have to play along with this fantasy world I believed he lived in. I knew it would be useless to threaten him, or argue with him, or appeal to his better nature. This would simply antagonise him, and I had no doubt from what Linus had told me that he could turn extremely nasty if anything was done which appeared to thwart him or disparage the nature of his business.

"From now on," I said, "I will make a point of locking up on every occasion. Thanks for the tip. Sorry it had to be repeated."

He chuckled. "I like your spirit."

He directed me to a road approaching a junction at the top on the Common, and I knew exactly where I was. Winstone's ice cream shop was clearly in view on my left. He required me to turn right then left into a private road leading to a number of substantial houses, and I eventually parked in the wide driveway of one of them, well out of sight of the road.

"Get out," he ordered, "and don't try anything silly. Lock the van – just to practise – and leave the keys in the lock. Then move away while I get them."

I followed his instructions with as good a grace as I could muster, and tried to appear relaxed about the whole thing.

We moved towards the house, and the door opened as we approached.

I tried not to show my surprise.

It was BMW Bastard. Obviously Russell had rescued him, and must have been aware all along that Emma and Linus were free.

"Surprise, eh?" he enquired.

"I would have expected nothing else," I replied, desperately trying to play it casual.

"Ah well, swings and roundabouts, swings and roundabouts. You can't have imagined I would not check with Nathan here, considering the importance of the people he was guarding? Now, will you please go into that room, which I use for an office and study, and sit down in that chair opposite my desk? I'm afraid I shall have to ask Nathan to tape you to it. He tells me that you know all about taping people to chairs, so this will come as no surprise to you. Don't worry. I've told him on no account to inflict any damage – unless you do anything silly, in which case I've given him a free hand. He said to tell you that would be a pleasure after what you did to him."

The note of menace was easily detectable beneath the suave *bonhomie*.

The room was large, and looked like a rather ornate office. Mullioned windows looked out over the side garden, which appeared to be part of extensive grounds. Behind me was a computer desk fitted with a range of monitors and printers, all very modern. In front of me was a heavy kneehole mahogany desk, probably Victorian in date. On the other side of the desk, facing me, was an executive leather chair, back to the wall, and on the desk itself were a couple of phones and a heavy desk light with enough flex to stretch anywhere it might be needed. The room smelt of leather and fresh coffee, and I detected the exotic aroma of the orchids flourishing on the window sill.

I was directed to a stout wooden chair, with upholstered seat and square wooden arms, and Nathan first taped my ankles to the chair with several turns of parcel tape, and then required me to place my right arm, wrist down, firmly on the chair while that too was taped.

I resignedly placed my left arm to await his attention, but Russell intervened.

"No," he said. "I want that arm taped wrist upwards."

Nathan pulled back my jacket sleeve and undid my shirt cuff, exposing my wrist, and taped my bare arm directly on to the chair.

"Oh, well, I suppose it makes for a little variety," I commented, trying to keep in part but wondering just exactly what he was playing at. Russell didn't seem to me to be the sort of person to do things without a reason.

"We'll see," he said. "We'll see." His tone had hardened.

"I need to go and check on a few things, like moving your van out of sight and making a few other arrangements. In the meantime, I suggest that you consider not only your problems, but perhaps you might like to consider mine as well. You know what I want. I had a deal with you, but you have not honoured your pledge. I therefore have to take other measures, and I imagine you have little doubt about my determination to get back what is, after all, mine.

"As you will have realised, I was well aware that you had somehow managed to release Miss Crawford and Linus, and I can only commend your enterprise. I respect initiative. Naturally, I expected some sort of a trap, which was why I sent a deputy to see if you actually did have the disc, and were carrying out your side of the arrangement. I was gratified to be informed that you did, indeed, have it, but disappointed that you should have attempted to intercept my deputy. I realised at once that I would have to take other measures to recover my disc, which I now believe is in the possession of your friends. I expected you to come back to your flat, and decided that we should renew our contract on different terms.

"I do not yet have a full report on what has happened at Egypt Mill, but I'll have it soon. We will then between us work out a recovery plan. I don't know whether or not you have involved the police, but it will still be necessary for you to find a way to return my property, and to return it to me quickly. Time is of the essence, and I am not prepared to compromise on this. If you can't think of a way to do so, then depend upon it, I will find one for you.

"So you have a good think. I will await a detailed report of what happened at Nailsworth, after which we can perhaps share our thoughts."

He sounded as though he was making a reasoned business proposal, of the sort Walmart might make to a corner shop owner. But the underlying menace was unmistakable. He left, locking the door. I had to admit to more confusion than I hoped I had shown him.

Chapter 15

I had some serious thinking to do, and I had to do it in a hurry, and do it right.

I was well aware that I had the disc burning a hole in my pocket all the time, and I could, of course, just give it to him and hope he would let me go. I considered this, but thought immediately that there were serious problems.

The first one was that he had now delivered me to what was obviously his home, or at least his headquarters. I was local, and he must realise that it was likely I knew exactly where I was. Even if I gave him the disc and he intended to cut and run, he would have to keep me prisoner while he made arrangements to leave and remove any evidence from the building. He couldn't afford to release me until he was well clear.

Even worse, he might think it preferable, once he had the disc safely back, to put me out of the way permanently. I could represent too much of a risk for his peace of mind.

Then again, if he got the disc and vanished with it, the whole point of our operation, which was to arrest him with the incriminating evidence in his possession, would be lost. Uncle Jim had insisted that we particularly wanted to have evidence to associate Russell personally with the disc, so I really needed to find some way in which we could achieve this primary aim.

I considered how Emma and Uncle Jim might be reacting. It would soon become obvious that I had been somehow intercepted since I had not returned in the expected ten minutes. It was now half an hour after I spoke to them, and they would surely guess that Russell had waylaid me. How would they react to this?

Well, Emma would no doubt say 'I told you so' and be anxious - with some justification, I ruefully thought - but Uncle Jim would think of practical possibilities. He would realise that Russell's priority would be the early recovery of the disc, and the most likely result of this would be that I'd have to convey some message about how it was to be returned. He would hope that Russell didn't know of the extent of police involvement, and that I would therefore contact Emma. With any luck, Uncle Jim would be able to put some sort of a trace on any calls to Emma's mobile, as that would be the most likely way for me to try to reach her. Russell would want to settle the matter as quickly as possible.

I couldn't guarantee any of this, of course, but I thought it seemed a reasonable scenario. It assumed I would be able to phone her, and depended upon what plans he demanded for the return of the disc.

The other thing that concerned me was how to engineer things so that Russell could be caught with the disc on him – something that Uncle Jim believed to be crucially important.

This was a real problem. The first objective was for me to get Emma to pretend to drop something which would look like the disc, and hope that Uncle Jim would find me before the deception was discovered. That would at least make it look as though I was co-operating, but I needed to make sure that Uncle Jim had as much time as possible to locate and rescue me, because if Russell found out that he had been duped - well, I'd rather not think about it. For this to work, I would have to make sure that Emma could guess where I was being held.

This was a risky strategy. If Russell made the pick-up and was arrested, then I have no doubt that Nathan would have instructions either to spirit me away, or inflict serious damage, or both. On the other hand, if Russell sent a minion to make the pick-up, Russell would remain clean. I needed to find some way in which I could associate Russell with the disc at the moment he was arrested.

A vague plan started to form in my mind, but the details would depend upon what Russell's instructions turned out to be.

I decided to go for it. If my plan didn't work out, and they didn't come for me in time, then I could always give in and hand over the disc – though what Russell's reaction to this would be I dreaded to think.

There was nothing more I could do. I had clarified in my own mind what my options were, but everything now depended upon what Russell proposed. I would just have to keep my wits about me and wing it.

Russell returned and seated himself in the chair behind the desk, facing me. He seemed to feel that this position gave him authority; and it did.

"Good," he said comfortably. "That's that settled. Your car is now well out of sight in the garage – and you'll be pleased to know that I locked it."

He grinned at me, and threw the keys on the table.

"Thanks," I replied. "You must have been a Boy Scout."

He laughed.

"OK, very funny." The smile disappeared, but the tone of reasonableness remained.

"You know perfectly well what I want, and I believe you can get it for me. In fact, we had a deal – a deal which you reneged on. Why did you not do as we arranged?"

"But I did," I insisted. "I put it exactly where you said, and left the building. I was going to the car park, and I saw this bloke panicking and making a dash across the mill race. He slipped and bashed his head. I think he was being taken to hospital, the last I saw of him."

Russell listened with attention. I felt he was convinced, at least for the moment.

"I assume he was your bloke. I didn't see what went on in the bar. I'd done as we agreed. If you didn't get your disc back, then it's hardly my fault."

For a moment he seemed uncertain.

"I don't want your bloody disc," I continued, pressing my advantage. "It's no earthly use to me. I found out where Emma was being kept by luck, and decided to rescue her. I don't like young ladies being abducted. Surely you can see that?"

"Go on," he said.

"Well, I'd got her back, and so as far as I'm concerned you can have your disc. I couldn't make head nor tail of it."

He pounced at once.

"You read it?" he demanded.

"Of course, I tried. I wanted to see what all the fuss was about. But I couldn't read it. It was in some language my computer couldn't access."

I could see doubt in his eyes. I felt I had stalled him for the moment. The phone rang, and he answered at once. He listened intently for a few moments.

"Go on," he said, "who else was there?"

When he put the phone down, his whole demeanour had changed. All doubt and uncertainty had disappeared.

"You have been telling me a load of porkies," he said, shaking his head in mock disappointment. "Oh, yes, it was mostly correct, what you said. It was what you didn't say that I'm interested in. For instance, you didn't say that Linus and Miss Crawford were waiting in the room above. You didn't say that there were several others lying in wait for my man – I don't yet know who they were, but they undoubtedly were there with evil intent. I don't yet know why my man aborted the pick up, but there must have been a very good reason. But what I'm mostly interested in is the fact that my man did not have the disc on him, and that it was not in the bar. I therefore conclude that one of your lot must have it. I want it back, and I want it now." He paused. "You are going to get it for me."

"What makes you so sure?" I wanted to know.

He paused a moment, heightening the suspense.

"What do you know about crack?" he asked

"Not a lot. Class A drug. Idiots use it."

"Very well put, if I may say so. Let me take it further. Crack has one particularly powerful characteristic: it very rapidly becomes addictive. Some people begin to feel addiction after one single trip, but for most it takes a few more – usually not more than six.

"After that, the one and only priority for the user is to get the next fix and the next fix usually needs to be larger and used more often. Believe me, my friend, I know about this.

"Once addiction has been established, the addict will do anything – and I mean anything – to get his next shot.

"Let me tell you how it is used. Crack is usually either smoked or snorted and is similar to cocaine but has two great advantages. First, it has a much lower vaporisation temperature – about 90 degrees centigrade - which means it can much more conveniently be smoked. Secondly, smoked crack can reach the brain in as little as eight seconds, so you can see why it is so popular, and is what I usually deal in. Cocaine is a different form of crack, has the same effect, but is less user-friendly because it is often injected as it vaporises at a much higher temperature – about 190 degrees. However, direct injection - mainlining - has one particular asset: it can be administered by another person." He stared intently at me.

"You may have wondered why I arranged for Nathan to tape your left wrist upwards. Well, I expect you can guess. It is so that I can get at the surface veins easily."

He paused to let the implication sink in. He needn't have bothered. I was way ahead of him, but this didn't help much. He continued relentlessly.

"You have two choices. Either you can contact your delightful Miss Crawford, and relay to her the instructions I shall give you, or else I shall start giving you a few cocaine trips. One advantage of injecting is that a trip doesn't last all that long – probably less than quarter of an hour. Then you would be more or less ready for another, and so on. After, say, five or six highs you will almost certainly be addicted. I can't be sure, because I've never tried it on this time-scale before, but my guess is that the craving will be overpowering. You will undoubtedly agree to anything I demand of you to get your next fix; so one way or another you will get that disc back for me."

He meant every word, and there was an awful logic about his scheme. He could see that I was impressed.

"I would like to think that you will cooperate fully this time. Remember this. I want that disc, and intend to have it. If I have to inject you to make you co-operate, then I will. Which is it to be? Cooperate – or cocaine?"

I opted to cooperate.

"Very wise, if I may say so.

"This is what I want you to do. You must persuade Miss Crawford to get hold of the disc. I am right in assuming she can do that?"

"Yes."

"Can you contact her?"

"Yes."

"How?"

"I have my mobile in my pocket, and her number is on it."

"Good. Tell her to wrap the disc in a waterproof package, and drop it at Tom Long's Post. Do you know where that is?"

"Yes."

"Will she know?"

"Quite possibly. But I can explain. It's obvious enough, in the middle of the crossroads on Minchinhampton Common. It's a special sign post."

"Exactly. It's right out in the open. There will be lots of people around, but not actually at the post itself, so it can be easily accessed. She is to drop it casually at the base and go. She is to do that exactly on the hour, and I will send someone up there to collect it. He will be watching the whole time; so will another of my men. Any attempt to follow or detain my man collecting the disc will have most unfortunate consequences for you. Do I make myself clear?"

"Abundantly," I said, thinking furiously how I would handle the call.

"When the disc is returned in an undamaged state, and I have verified this, you will be taken in your van to a suitable spot and left there. I'm afraid you will be tied up, for we need time to make some personal arrangements; however, I shall arrange for your location to be known when I am ready, and you will be released. You have my word that I shall keep my part of the bargain providing you keep yours."

He sounded plausible enough but I couldn't help thinking that if he did get the disc back he might very well think that I was too great a risk to let go.

"OK, I'll make the call. Is it all right if I arrange the drop for three o'clock? She won't have time to make it earlier."

"I agree. To have it returned by then would be a satisfactory outcome for both of us."

"I shall need to have my right hand free if I am to use my mobile," I pointed out.

He paused for a moment.

"I don't see why not. I will get Nathan to release it – but you won't mind me covering you with my little gun here just to make sure you don't get any silly ideas into your head, will you?"

"You overestimate me," I replied.

He looked at me for a moment.

"No," he said. "No. I don't think I do. That's why I shall have the gun."

He went to fetch Nathan. I had a few precious moments to collect my wits and think how I could tip Emma off exactly where I was – and hope that Uncle Jim would act as the US Cavalry.

I needed to keep the call going as long as possible. If they had thought of putting a trace on phone calls, it would help in confirming the source. If I could think of some way in which I could tip Emma off about where I was it might also help.

I racked my brains. I also thought it might be useful if I could somehow get myself free from the constricting grip of the tapes binding me. I noticed that my left arm was exposed and bound actually on my skin; but my right arm was bound tight over my jacket sleeve. It was still securely attached to the arm of the chair, but I had the glimmering of an idea of how I could make use of that fact. It would all depend upon how awake Nathan was. I thought I might be in with a chance.

I had just thought how I could get a coded message to Emma when Russell returned, trailing a surly-looking Nathan behind him.

Chapter 16

Russell produced a gun, and levelled it at me.

"Just do as you're told, and there need be no unpleasantness. I said I didn't underestimate you; don't you underestimate me." The menace had returned to his voice.

"Where is your phone?"

"In my inside jacket pocket."

"You know what you have got to say? She is to drop the packet at Tom Long's Post at exactly three o'clock. She must then leave. Any attempt to intercept or follow the person picking it up will be observed, with serious repercussions for you. You must impress upon her that we are not playing games, and that any deviation from my conditions will have some of the unfortunate results that I have outlined to you. When I have the disc, and I have verified that it is authentic, you will be taken to another location and left there; and when I am ready your colleague will be informed.

"Any questions?"

"No."

"OK, Nathan, cut the tape on his right arm."

Nathan produced a craft knife, and slit my bonds.

"Now, very slowly get your mobile out."

I flexed my fingers for a moment or two as though to relieve some stiffness, undid the two buttons of my jacket, and slowly pulled out my mobile.

"That's very good." Russell was now sounding almost patronising. "Now ring Miss Crawford."

The critical moment had come. I would have to assume that much of the conversation would be overheard by Russell, so I had to be on my guard. So would Emma. I turned my mobile on and pressed Emma's number. The response was almost immediate.

"Oliver?" I could hear the concern in her voice.

"Yes. It's OK. I'm all right. But I want you to listen to me, and not ask any questions. It is important that you do exactly as I ask. I'm sure you can guess why."

"I'm being held as security for the return of the disc that all the fuss has been about. Any failure to do as we are told will lead to me being turned into a drug addict – or worse, if that is possible. We cannot afford to mess up on this. Is that clear?"

There was a short pause "Yes," she said unsteadily.

"You know where the disc is at the moment?"

She paused again, puzzled.

"Yes… but."

"But nothing," I quickly cut her off. "I need you to make up a small package with the disc inside, and put it where I tell you. Will you do that?"

There was yet another pause while she worked out exactly what I meant.

"Yes," she said, still puzzled.

Come on, Emma, I thought. Perhaps I should feed in the time factor.

"It is important that you drop it at exactly three o'clock. That should give you enough time, shouldn't it?"

I caught a faint 'Yes' in the background from her end.

"Yes, it should." She sounded much more positive now.

"You have to drop it at a particular place. I don't suppose you know Tom Long's Post, not being local."

There was a pause. I wanted to string the conversation out as long as possible in order for any trace to have a reasonable chance. I just hoped she would catch on.

"No," she said, catching on. "Never heard of it."

"Well, it's in the middle of Minchinhampton Common."

"Where's that?"

"Well, you know if you go up the hill to Rodborough Common…"

"…I get to Stroud." she said. I was proud of her.

"No, no, no, that's going the other way. You need to go along the top, away from Stroud, towards Cirencester."

"I thought you said Minchinhampton."

"I did. Just listen, will you? I want you to go up the hill to Rodborough Common. Have you got that?

"Yes."

"Then take the road towards Minchinhampton, which is just further along the road that eventually leads to Cirencester. Before you get to Minchinhampton, you come to Minchinhampton Common. There, you will find a crossroads. You can't miss it, and by this crossroads there is a signpost standing out all by itself. That is called Tom Long's Post."

"How will I be able to tell?" she asked innocently.

"You can tell because there is a sign at the top saying Tom Long's Post."

I had my reasons for sounding like an impatient male patronisingly explaining directions to a useless female. I heard a suppressed giggle coming from the other end.

I took heart. So far the plan seemed to be working.

"Can I park there?" she enquired.

"Oh yes, there is a parking space just off to the right. Don't try and park anywhere else or you may get a golf ball through your windscreen. There's a public golf course up there.

"Anyway, drop the package at the base of the post at exactly three o'clock, and then drive right away, and another thing, don't get any of the lads to try to follow the person who picks it up – if they do, the whole deal is off, and I shall be made to suffer for it.

"I'd rather not suffer, so you be a good girl and do exactly as I ask, and when it's all over I will pop across to the shop and buy you your favourite double rum and raisin, no flake. Is that a deal?"

There was a short pause.

"That would be lovely," she said.

I hoped that my patronising tone would sound as authentic to Russell as it would sound contrived to Emma.

"Anyway, as soon as the package has been delivered and verified, I will be driven in my van to a secret location. When they are ready – which I imagine will be after three or four hours...." I looked at Russell, and he nodded ".... you will be informed of where I am, and can come and get me. I'm not sure how you will be informed, but I have their word that you will be.

"Then all this stupid business will be over and we can get back to normal."

"I can't wait," she said. "Now, shall I just go over that again, to make sure I've got it right? I don't want to make any mistakes."

Emma, you are brilliant, I decided. She had clearly picked the nuances that I had hoped to convey, and I was sure she would deduce that I was somewhere close to Winstone's. And I was absolutely sure that Uncle Jim would be making the most of the opportunity to locate my call, which would give him plenty of time to effect a rescue before Russell discovered our duplicity.

I could hardly contain my excitement while she slowly recapped the instructions I had given her, making one or two mistakes, which I could correct with apparently flagging patience.

Eventually I rang off.

"Women," I said despairingly to Russell.

"You did very well. Congratulations. I hope we can maintain this level of co-operation. Strange as it may seem to you, I don't enjoy violence. It is just that it becomes necessary sometimes."

I made a move to replace my mobile.

"No," he said. "Don't turn it off; just put it on the desk. When I have the disc, I'll take your phone with me and redial the number you have just rung. That is how I can arrange for your release."

At least he seemed to be prepared to keep his side of the bargain. Fortunately, he had no idea that I wasn't prepared to keep mine.

"Nathan, tape up his arm again. I'm taking no chances."

Nathan approached the desk and picked up the parcel tape.

What happened next might be critical.

I put my elbow resignedly on the wooden arm of the chair, and dropped my hand down, sliding my elbow an inch or two further back as I did so. I cocked my wrist up, as though my whole hand fell over the end of the armrest.

However, by sliding further back, the end of the armrest now came into the palm of my hand. I braced my arm so that it felt solid against the chair, even though it was in reality half an inch or so above it. The gap was masked by the sleeve of my jacket. I just hoped that Nathan would assume I would once more be firmly secured to the chair.

As he started to replace the bonds I kept my arm firmly braced to preserve the gap. Nathan didn't notice.

"He won't get out of that," he sneered to Russell, and replaced the tape and the knife on the desk.

Well, I thought, we'll see about that. You may be right. But if I get an even break and a bit of time to myself I might just have a try. For the moment, though, I had to keep my arm braced to prevent any slack appearing in my bonds.

Nathan left, and Russell obviously had more business with me. He sat back in his chair.

"I admire your spirit, but I have to say that you have caused me a great deal of trouble. I can only hope for your sake that this current arrangement works as well as it should, because if it doesn't – well, I may well run out of patience."

"As it is, I am obliged to move out of this particular residence, and that is largely your fault. Fortunately for you, I can well afford to move as I have other places from which I can operate. None the less, since I am confidently expecting to have what I need in a little over an hour, I shall have to make some arrangements to clear up here before departure."

"That means I shall have to leave you for a bit. I don't think you will be foolish enough to try to escape, even if you could. I have men outside who will have no hesitation in taking whatever action is necessary to prevent you – and they are not so sensitive to violence as I am, so be warned."

"Still, I think it is advisable to give you something to keep you occupied while I am checking things outside. I told you a little bit about crack, cocaine and the effects they have a few moments ago."

"Yes. I remember very well," I said, dreading what I felt sure would come next.

"Possibly you didn't believe me," he said intently, enjoying his position of dominance. "Well, now's your chance to find out for certain."

There was nothing I could do, and he knew it.

I had never done drugs, and never wanted to; and, after hearing about Steve and Linus' father, I could see compelling reasons not to.

Yet I knew it would be useless trying to appeal to his better nature; and to struggle and protest would simply give him an even greater satisfaction than he had at the moment. Whether his motive was for revenge, or to keep me occupied while he was otherwise engaged, I would never know.

The only thing that was clear was that he intended to inject me.

I was even more shaken than he realised. It was difficult to maintain the *façade* of forced *bonhomie* that I had managed up till then, but I was anxious not to appear as defeated or frightened as I felt.

"You'd better get on with it, then," I said heavily.

He looked at me.

"Have you done drugs before?" he asked.

"No."

"Then cheer up, you may even like it. Many people do. I wouldn't be in business if they didn't. It isn't as bad as some people make out – in fact, a number of medicinal products use it with excellent results. The trouble is people are so prejudiced."

He almost sounded plausible, as though he was doing me some sort of favour. I could have pointed out that arsenic is also used in some medical products, but I didn't think it was the time. In fact, I could think of nothing to say at all, as any further comment from me was likely to make matters worse. It was quite clear what was going to happen, and there was nothing I could do to prevent it.

I clung on to the fervent hope that one dose was unlikely to have any permanent effect, wondering how many eventual addicts had thought the same.

He continued in a conversational way as he produced a phial of liquid and a syringe.

"This is straight cocaine, of course, but it has much the same effect as crack. I won't give you too large a shot since you're not used to it. I expect it will last ten minutes at the most. Don't worry this is the genuine article, not polluted with dangerous additives such as some of the less scrupulous dealers provide."

He was beginning to sound like a professional service provider, with a real concern for his clients. Perhaps he even saw himself in that light.

"And this is a new needle. You will only feel a slight jab, because new needles are sharp. You should see the results of blunt needles, quite shocking."

He inserted the needle in the top of the phial.

"Also, this needle is sterilised. It is very dangerous to use unsterilised needles, and especially to re-use them. I never recommend it."

He seemed incapable of understanding why anyone would choose to use blunt or dirty needles. The fact that they were forced to behave like that as a result of the habit he promoted simply did not occur to him. Their behaviour was their fault, not his.

He withdrew the needle, squirted a little liquid into the air with the professional medical gesture, and moved over to me.

I braced myself. He took hold of my left hand and examined my upturned wrist for a suitable place to inject.

"You will hardly feel anything," he said with professional reassurance, and inserted the needle.

He was right. I didn't. He slowly emptied the syringe, and then withdrew it. He dabbed the entry point with disinfectant and cotton wool.

"I'll leave you now," he said casually. "I'll lock the door to make sure you are not disturbed." He picked up his gear and made towards the door.

"Oh, yes," he said as he placed the key in the far side of the door and reappeared in the doorway for a moment.

"I know that you are not actually going anywhere, but I think it might be appropriate to wish you a good trip."

As an attempt at humour, I thought it left a lot to be desired. I was left sitting by myself, wondering how on earth I had been reduced to a state of spending a Sunday afternoon bound to a chair, about to take a Class A trip, and hoping beyond hope that my reasoning would work; that my plans were not as flimsy as they momentarily seemed; that I had not just imagined that Emma had fully understood my coded conversation; that Uncle Jim had been able to get a fix on where I was and would be able to reach me in time; that Russell would not discover my duplicity too soon.

Then I thought of the appalling nature of the racket that Russell was so urbanely organising, and the fact that there were probably thousands of young people like Steve who had been driven to despair or permanently damaged by Russell's deadly regime; and my resolve hardened.

If Russell and his whole operation could be smashed, then it was worth it, even if it meant me taking a drug-induced trip. The only disturbing thing was I had no idea how I would cope with what was about to happen.

Chapter 17

At first, nothing happened at all. I felt completely normal. Apprehensive, but normal I reviewed the position so far.

I convinced myself that Emma had realised what was going on, at least most of it. The muffled 'yes' to my question about 'enough time' clearly implied that Uncle Jim could get some sort of a fix on me, and it certainly would take him less than an hour to set up a rescue. Also, Emma was definitely playing along with the idea of keeping the conversation flowing. I was sure she knew where Tom Long's Post was – everyone with local knowledge did – and her pretended ignorance only confirmed my view. As for the Stroud touch – and the rehash of my over-complicated directions – well, I took my hat off to her. I decided she deserved a seriously big kiss.

I was equally sure that she had taken on board the 'double rum and raisin' comment; if so, she would undoubtedly have an almost exact knowledge of the area within which I must be held.

I had relaxed my right arm and, as I had hoped, there was now quite a reasonable amount of play in the restricting tape. I was able to work my arm sideways and up and down in the hope that I could twist the stuff to breaking point. The bands undoubtedly moved and gave even more latitude, but unfortunately they tended to twist together and form into a strong rope which I knew I had no hope of breaking. It had been a good idea, but it just didn't work. Still, I felt I could look forward to being rescued. I felt very optimistic about the outcome.

In fact, I was beginning to feel very optimistic about everything. It seemed as though the worries of the world were gently fading away, and I realised that the cocaine had begun to take over.

It was an extraordinary feeling. It was difficult to explain fully, except to say that I suddenly began to feel like a small boy waking up on Christmas morning. There was a feeling of excitement, of happy anticipation, of euphoric expectation, which erased any sense of apprehension or concern. I suddenly felt absolutely certain that all my reasoning had been right, and was bound to work. I had absolute confidence that Uncle Jim would have located the site of my call, and was even now about to rescue me. I thought he would walk in the door at any moment. Emma would be with him, and we would have a glorious few moments in each other's arms while Uncle Jim impounded Russell's empire. Nothing could go wrong.

I became particularly aware of my senses. I looked with fascination at the books on the shelf. I almost felt the greenness of the green ones, the redness of the red, and the clarity of the gold lettering of their titles. It seemed as though I could feel their squareness and their weight. I gazed at the glowing grain of the polished mahogany items of furniture, sensing their warmth and solidity. I seemed to be able to focus on each silken thread of the heavy damask curtains hung lustrously by the sash windows.

I listened intently to the ticking of the coach clock on the mantelpiece across the room. I had, I suppose, been aware of it all along, but now I *noticed* it, in the same way that I noticed the birdsong outside the window and the sound of boxes being moved somewhere outside.

I felt warm, and my heart beat faster as though I had been running for a while. By now, my eyes seemed to take in all sorts of details that usually are taken for granted or casually by-passed without attention. I saw the parcel tape and the craft knife lying on the desk where Nathan had left them. I took in the heavy table lamp and the long plastic cord, which ran from it; it reminded me of a lasso or a noose. I looked at the desk itself – heavy, solid mahogany, drawers front and back. I focussed on the brass knobs, which seemed to sparkle in their polished fronts.

I surveyed the whole room in this manner, amazed that I had not previously noticed half of the things I now saw with great clarity. The feeling of euphoria remained.

I was pleasantly surprised to find that my mind, far from being fuddled with dope as I had expected, was crystal clear. I knew that what I saw was the result of the drug. I knew that the feelings of awareness were both pleasurable and somehow inspiring, but I was also fully aware that there was a price to be paid for these moments of chemically induced pleasure. I could understand the attraction for people who needed to escape from themselves, but I also knew that the cost of doing so was prohibitive. A moment's consideration of Steve or Linus' father demonstrated that fact for me beyond any argument. I thought it was time to stop being intrigued by the experience, and concentrate on my main objective.

I realised that the effect was wearing off. I looked about me once more while my state of awareness remained high. I had not lost the will to do anything I could to outwit Russell, or to make it easier for my rescuers to achieve their aim. I decided that what I really needed to do was to free myself from the chair.

I stared at the tape binding me. There was nothing I could do about my legs, so it would have to be the arms. With great intensity I scrutinised my left arm, wrist up and tightly bound. However hard I looked, I could see no way in which I could wriggle free. There was no leverage here and even with the advantage of some leeway the other arm had remained secure. I knew, because I'd tried.

I looked at my right arm again as my feeling of optimism began to disappear.

The tape had been bound round the bottom of the sleeve of my jacket. It was true that I had achieved some looseness, some wriggle-room; but I had tested this, and only succeeded in twisting the tape into an even stronger bond. I had hoped that I might be able to twist or stretch the tape so that I could pull my arm free, but it just didn't work. Of course, there was still some slack – I could move my wrist up to an inch above the armrest, letting the loose sleeve dangle below it – but I could not see a way to make use of this.

I stared intently at the sleeve, and my arm within. In my imaginative frame of mind, the sleeve reminded me of a tunnel.

A tunnel! Things move through tunnels – but the tunnels themselves stay still.

I shifted my body as far round to the left as I could and, leaving the sleeve strapped where it was, tried to ease my arm out. I couldn't quite make it, because the back of the chair prevented my arm from sliding out.

I needed to get my shoulder out of my jacket. Thank heaven I had undone the front buttons when I reached for my phone, because this gave me a chance. By wriggling my right shoulder against the back of the chair, I gradually worked the right-hand side of the jacket down behind my back. Once it was there, it was only a moment's work to slip my whole arm out of the sleeve.

Instantly I reached for the craft knife on the desk, and was about to cut myself free when I paused for a second.

What was I actually trying to achieve?

If I simply freed myself, what would I then do? Russell had made it clear that he had men outside and they had no doubt been told to use any means to stop me; therefore escape would be difficult. Also, if he knew I had escaped, he would be warned and disappear; he would not be arrested with the disc. On the other hand, if he thought I was still taped up, he would be entirely off his guard; and I thought could see a way to overcome him and plant the disc on him as well. I thought it was a risk worth taking.

I carefully cut the tapes binding my left wrist in a straight line against the underside of the armrest, setting my arm free. Then I repeated the process on my right sleeve, gently peeling the tapes from the armrest. It was a simple task to release my ankles in the same way, cutting the tapes at the back.

Having freed myself, I practised doing myself up again. I wanted to be able to free myself at will, but give the impression of still being secured. If I could replace the cut edges of the tape and re-stick them on the wood of the chair, the illusion would be complete.

I tried it once or twice, but the tapes retained too much adhesion for a clean escape. Fortunately, the more times I tried, the less adhesion remained – and in the end I could arrange for the tapes to appear to be intact, but be able to break them in an instant. I did the same with my arm bands, and ended up with a manageable product. They would not stand a close scrutiny, but then I wasn't expecting one.

Before I replaced the tapes for the final time, I had one more task. The long flex for the lamp came round the front of the desk from below, and I pulled through as much as I thought I would need. I made a careful calculation and then knotted a section of it to two of the brass knobs on the front drawers nearest to me on my right. Then I replaced the lamp more or less where it had been, but marginally nearer to me.

This was the weakest part of my plan. If it was noticed, then my whole charade would collapse in an instant. However, I had two things going in my favour. The two drawers were immediately by my right side, and were therefore covered from view – I expected Russell to approach his desk from the left, as he had done previously. Next, he couldn't possibly expect me to have broken my bonds simply to remain where I was. In any case, he would have other things on his mind, and would hardly be looking for this sort of stratagem.

I had a final look round, checking everything I could think of. It all looked fine to me.

I sat myself in the chair and carefully replaced the tapes round my ankles. I thought they looked convincing enough. Next, I repeated the process on my left arm, and this also achieved a satisfactory result.

Then I dealt with my right arm. I put the two ends of the cut tapes together, stuck loosely to the side of the armrest, and then manoeuvred my arm through the resulting tunnel. It proved impossible to achieve this without dislodging the semi-stuck tapes.

This proved to be a real nuisance. I tried it with my jacket fully on to start with, but couldn't make enough room to ease my arm through. With the jacket off my shoulder it was easier, but I found the movement necessary to wriggle my jacket back up again invariably burst the tapes open.

It was hopeless. My right arm was the most obvious of all, a dead give-away if anything was wrong with the bonding.

I had to do something, and do it quickly. It was a question of priorities. My right arm *had* to look properly bound, so something else would have to be sacrificed.

I released both my arms, and undid the binding on my right ankle. I wound the cut tapes round my ankle, ignoring the chair leg altogether. I secured my left arm as before, and put my jacket on. The tapes were loosely sticking out from the right sleeve, and I carefully positioned my arm to where it had been. Then I raised my free right leg and with my knee carefully pressed the loose tapes into position on the armrest.

It wasn't perfect, but it would have to do. I put my right ankle back against the chair leg, and hoped that Russell would not feel the need to inspect me too closely.

I surveyed my preparations. I had a clear idea of what I intended to do and it had seemed quite logical. However, by this time the effect of the drug was beginning to wear off – and I started to have doubts.

Surely he would notice there was something different? Surely he would see the lamp had been moved – and I could be the only person to have done it? Surely he would want to check my bonds after leaving me alone for a while? He had said clearly that he didn't underestimate me – so wouldn't that be the first thing he would think of?

In this mood, the certainty of my rescue seemed less persuasive. There were a number of houses in the area, which could have fitted the clues – supposing Uncle Jim could not find the right one? What would happen if Russell discovered he had been duped before Uncle Jim could reach me?

Doubts crowded in on me. I half realised that this anxiety might be caused by the after-effects of the drug, misgivings replacing blithe confidence; but it didn't make it any less worrying. I wondered if I had done the sensible thing in setting up this elaborate scheme to entrap Russell.

I realised it was too late to do anything else now – I'd committed myself to my plan. I just felt it probably wouldn't work. I needed to pull myself together. I thought of Linus and Steve, and my attitude hardened.

I thought of how Russell had treated me a few nights ago – and how he was treating me now, for heaven's sake – and I felt I was doing the right thing.

I thought of what he had done, and what he had threatened to do to Emma; and my mind was fully made up. This was just as well, because at that moment I heard the key turn in the lock as Russell returned.

Chapter 18

Russell sauntered into the room. I tried to look as though I accepted my fate, hoping that nothing would alert him to my activities. Fortunately, he only gave me a casual glance, understandably assuming everything was how he left it.

As I hoped, he made directly for his chair, and settled himself comfortably into it, resting his arms on the desk. He looked at me.

"How did you get on?" he asked conversationally.

"With the trip? Well, I suppose it was ….. interesting."

"Yes, I'm sure it was. That's what everyone says. I never use the stuff myself. Not my scene."

"No, it's not mine either," I replied.

"Very wise, if I may say so." He sounded like a concerned uncle. "It always surprises me that some people are prepared to pay such a high price for such temporary pleasure. Socrates would have been shocked."

He seemed to revel in demonstrating his public school upbringing by effortless references to the classics. I could only assume that he felt it gave him an air of respectability.

"Socrates preferred hemlock," I replied grimly, thinking that Linus' father had preferred death to living intolerably.

"Very good," he said, genuinely impressed that someone else could play the suave intellectual bit with him. "Very good. I appreciate a civilised conversation." He stared at me for a full minute, examining my face for reaction.

"You know," he said conversationally, "I gave you that shot just to let you know that I could – and would, if necessary. I am sure one shot won't hurt you, but you must understand that I can take no chances. I applaud your attitude to drugs – I share it myself. I never take them, and never have. Don't start."

I felt this was rich coming from him. What had he just tried to do – and what would he do if the rescue misfired? I needed to keep him talking.

"Yet you are quite happy supplying others?" I asked.

"Quite happy. What other people choose to do is up to them. They are mostly young people who use it. Either they are youngsters trying it out – and why shouldn't they – they will probably get a few kicks before giving it up, if they have enough sense not to get addicted. Alternatively, they are losers, and they will be losers whether they do drugs or not. How they afford it is up to them. If they don't get it from me, they would get it from somewhere else. Why not from me?"

"I've had a good education, but I'm not in the first academic rank and all the careers that my peers seem to enjoy bore me rigid. I'm not a nine-to-five person. What I do gives me a fairly small but stimulating element of danger for a remarkably good return. Just look around you. I've several houses like this. I'm doing much better than most of my more academically gifted contemporaries."

I forbore to point out that what they did was probably legal, and did not involve easing vulnerable youngsters into a life of addiction, crime and despair.

"What about the possibility of getting caught?"

"What about it? It's that possibility that keeps my wits up to scratch. It adds spice to life, stimulates the mind, and there is an immense pleasure in keeping ahead of the authorities. That is why there is no way I am going to let that disc get away from me."

I decided not to say that the disc had already got away from him, and that its contents were even now allowing the police to build a watertight case against his whole operation.

"No, I realise that. What was on the disc, anyway?" I asked conversationally, choosing to let him keep his illusions a little longer. He couldn't help showing off.

"Oh, just my whole operation accounts, personnel, contacts. It was a very special disc, one that you have probably not come across. I'm not surprised you couldn't read it. You were not supposed to. Nobody can, apart from me."

He frowned, remembering something.

"And Linus. He's probably told you. Fortunately, he can do nothing without the disc in his possession – which is another reason why I have to have it back."

He seemed sufficiently sure of himself to continue to confide in me.

"I can also do without his signature. I can get that copied easily enough, though he doesn't believe I can. Still, I owe him one; he has double-crossed me when I trusted him. I won't have people doing that to me."

I was amazed at his reasoning. It did not occur to him that Linus owed him one for causing the death of his father. Apparently, in Russell's world, grudges were borne and retribution dealt out solely in one direction. I felt I had to keep him talking amiably in case he discovered my duplicity.

"No," I responded, "Nobody likes to be taken in by those you think you can trust. I can quite see that."

He gave my face another penetrating scrutiny.

"You know, I could use you. You seem to understand. You have shown yourself to be resourceful and practical – I like that. I gather you are some sort of engineer. How much do you earn?"

"A bit over thirty thousand."

"Thirty thousand? You come and join me and you could earn at least four times that amount – and that's in the first year. After that, the sky's the limit. Think about it."

It didn't require much thought. At the moment, I was doing something I was good at, something I enjoyed, something which was of undoubted use to others, something which offered me a solid, worthwhile future, something I could live on comfortably and it was legal.

Russell was offering me the opportunity for huge personal profit, but one, which degraded other people, which would undoubtedly involve me in treating some clients or desperate employees with contempt and brutality, and which offered the prospect of long periods in prison and social ostracism.

I tried to prevent the contempt I had for his proposal from showing on my face, but I was finding it increasingly difficult to maintain the *façade* of genial banter with this warped entrepreneur.

Where was Uncle Jim?

It suddenly dawned on me that Russell thought of himself as some sort of professional, and took a pride in what he did for a living. He had compared himself favourably to some of his more talented peers, and from this he seemed to draw justification. I thought it couldn't do any harm to get him to discuss his operating methods – this would keep him talking about his favourite subject, and might well be of assistance to Uncle Jim later on. I pretended to be considering his proposition.

"That's a lot of money," I mused.

"I thought you might be impressed."

"What exactly would it involve?"

"Well," he said, warming to the subject, "You don't have to do any of the actual dealing. I get others to do that."

I was well aware of it.

"Your role would be an administrative one. I make the supplier contacts, but it needs someone to arrange for delivery and, of course, payment that can be quite a complicated and ever-changing operation, requiring considerable organisational skills. I always keep supplies in small amounts in a variety of different places. This is an obvious precaution. None of my operatives know each other, just their own patch. If one of my men gets caught, it does not affect the rest of the organisation. It is the same with money. Everything that comes in to me is in fairly small amounts, partly because this does not attract questions, and partly because if someone is busted it makes very little difference to the whole. But I am sure you can see that this takes a talent for organisation, and this is getting to be a burden, which I would like to share. I have every confidence that someone like you could do it."

He sounded like a personnel officer attracting a key new executive. I was glad he could not read my mind. I dropped my head, as though in thought. I was horror-struck.

The lower strands of tape on my sleeve had become detached from the arm of my chair, and were now waving in mid-air. At all costs I had to try to keep his gaze away from there until I was ready.

"Where would I work from?" I asked desperately trying to keep the anxiety out of my voice.

"Oh, that's no problem. At the moment I work from here, but I have several other offices as required. It sometimes becomes necessary to move location, so I keep my options open."

I turned my head to the office area behind me.

"What systems do you use?"

He seemed pleased at my interest. He got out of his chair and strolled to the workstation, where he proceeded to give me a run-down on his operation.

It was fortunate that he appeared to be something of a geek, taking a huge pride in his gear, and wishing to impress me with the fact that he only used the latest, most sophisticated and expensive equipment. He began to enthuse about his operative practices, and I was able to make appreciative responses to some of his more pertinent observations. He certainly knew about computer systems.

Fortunately, so did I, and he seemed to take a boyish delight in finding someone who appreciated the excellence of his undertaking. I had to admit I was impressed. I found myself thinking it was a real shame that such a deadly cause should be supported by such a sophisticated enterprise.

I kept him talking for a while, desperately wondering what I could do to prevent him realising my bonds had been broken. I wondered about trying to use my knee again to push back the errant strands, but I thought this would be far too obvious; he would inevitably notice. I tried to let my jacket fall open to cover the arm, but there was no way it would stay there unless I adopted a totally unnatural pose.

I received a brief reprieve when the door opened and Nathan stuck his head inside.

"The van's here," he announced. "What exactly is to go?"

This occupied both of them for a few minutes more, and involved taking some of the more important pieces from the workbench. Russell directed the removals with a quiet efficiency, and then said genially, "I've a few things to do outside. Don't go away," and he locked the door.

Enormously relieved, I kneed the dangling tapes back into some sort of position. By this time they had lost much of their original adhesion, and it was a real problem trying to make the join look authentic. I was afraid they might come apart again at any time, and was only too aware that my whole strategy depended upon Russell not realising what I was up to.

I was now seriously concerned about what he would do if he found out what my real intentions were. I had played him along, pretending to consider his proposition when I had nothing but contempt for it, and appearing interested in his enthusiastic description of his equipment and methods when my only interest was to gain information which could be used against him. But most important of all, I had treated him as an equal, as a successful businessman; I had applauded his technical knowledge, and allowed our mutual interests to appear to form a basis of respect for each other.

It would come as a huge blow to his self-esteem if he realised that this was all a complete sham – and that he had fallen for it. Far from having any respect for him, the more I saw of him the more I loathed him and his whole lethal business; and he would instantly realise this if he discovered my real intentions.

How he would react to such a discovery I dreaded to think. He certainly would not be pleased. He had made it abundantly clear what he thought about people who, in his terms, betrayed his trust.

I was not merely betraying his trust – I was playing him for a complete sucker. I just hoped I was up to it, because I guessed it would either be him or me.

Russell returned, still in a genial mood, and settled once more in his chair.

"I was quite serious about my proposition just now. I feel sure I could value the qualities of someone like you. After the dust has died down a little, shall I contact you? I know where you live."

I hardly knew what to say. If I said what I felt he would have a fit, but I didn't want to antagonise him. I hesitated, as though giving the matter some thought.

"Well, you can try. But I have to warn you, I very much like what I am doing at the moment. It's what I have trained for."

"You must, of course, please yourself. But if you ever get to the point where you feel you might be making more in the world, you may change your mind. I'll probably give you a call in a year's time – then we'll see if your enthusiasm for the conventional has remained intact."

"Well, it shouldn't be long now. My men are out on the common, and they have their instructions. Miss Crawford has had plenty of time to do as requested. Provided she does as she was told, then we can complete the deal. Do you have any problems? Is there any way she is going to do anything silly?"

"No," I said, "I have every confidence in her. I'm sure she will do as I indicated – assuming she can find Tom Long's Post," I added in a condescending tone, for which I hoped Emma would forgive me.

"Good. As soon as I have the disc back, we shall leave. We will go in your car, and you will be secured as I told you. Do you need to go to the toilet before we go? You might not have another chance for several hours."

His consideration did him credit. Unfortunately, for me to accept would mean the inevitable discovery of my broken bonds, and I just couldn't let that happen, not at this late hour.

"No, I shall be fine. Thanks for your consideration."

I thought I had managed to keep the concern out of my voice, but I clearly hadn't managed it.

Russell looked at me closely. I returned his stare, but I could sense his manner change. I obviously wasn't as good a liar as I had hoped.

Knowing where my problem lay, I thoughtlessly glanced down at my bound right sleeve.

The whole bottom section had come free, and was flapping idly below the armrest. He followed my gaze. He froze.

"So. We've been playing games, have we? That, my friend, was a serious mistake." He leaned forward.

Chapter 19

It was the chance I had been hoping for. Before he could understand what was happening, I shook my ankles clear of the chair-legs and at the same instant pulled both arms free.

Kicking the chair out of the way, I braced my weight against the front of the desk and pushed with every ounce of strength I had.

The whole thing seemed unwilling to move, but suddenly it slid backwards trapping Russell and his chair against the wall. His legs were pinned under the desk.

The movement of the desk had caught him unawares, and he received a blow in his midriff, which temporarily winded him, and he doubled up.

I grabbed the length of electric cable from the lamp with my left hand and wound it twice round his neck, crossing it over so that he could not wriggle out of it. I had thought that the weight of the lamp might be enough to keep him secure, but I decided not to risk it, and hitched the rest of the flex to the drawer knobs on the left hand side.

All this happened remarkably quickly, and I had the wit to remove the knife and anything else that may have been of use out of the reach of Russell's free arms.

Russell was incandescent; but fear also showed on his face.

I tightened the flex constricting his neck.

"Don't talk," I said, "or it will be the last thing you do".

There didn't seem any point in civilities.

While he was still disorientated, surprised, and furious, I made a dart for the door. But instead of letting myself out, I locked it from within. It was a stout door, and would at least prevent Nathan from reappearing.

The initial stages over, I surveyed my handiwork. Russell was hogtied. His chair was pressed against the wall, and kept there by the weight of the heavy desk, while he himself was bent forwards over the top of the desk with cord wound round his neck securing him there. I had considered how he might extricate himself from this position, but it was impossible, especially with his body bent over the desktop and his legs trapped in the kneehole area. There was no way in which he could exert the necessary leverage to shift the heavy piece, and any attempt to straighten up resulted in strangulation. He was well and truly stuck.

The only problem I could foresee was that he might be able partially to open one of the drawers on his side and find some implement he could use against me. He had left the gun on the workbench behind me, but I couldn't take the risk. I pulled on the flex and it tightened. He gasped.

"Keep your hands flat on the desk top where I can see them, or I will pull the flex tighter," I ordered. "Do you understand?"

He nodded, gasping. He placed his hands where I told him, and I relaxed the flex a little. I quickly picked up the chair I had kicked over, and sat myself down opposite Russell. I put my hand on the flex to give me instant control over the tension.

I hoped that Uncle Jim would hurry up. I'd seen no sign of him so far, so I needed to prevent Russell having time to think; I had no illusions about his ruthlessness and resourcefulness. I decided to treat him to a sermon in the manner of his own pompous self-justification, which I hoped would not only annoy and distract him, but also allow me to say a few things for my own satisfaction. He tried to speak.

"Shut up," I said, giving the flex a tweak.

He shut up. There was a look of desperation in his eyes.

"We will only have to wait a few minutes at the most. As you yourself said, the operation is nearly over, but not in the way you meant.

"Miss Crawford does not have the disc. She will do the drop as arranged, but with a dummy package. Your men will be intercepted as they try to recover it, and any others will be arrested when they return here. They will not be able to inform you of their capture and in any case, as you realise, you will not be in a position to resort to your habitual violence as a method of getting your own way.

"At any moment, the narcotics squad, who have been in on the whole business from the start, will be here in force. They have discovered precisely where you are operating from, and are already on their way."

I didn't actually know this because I had been forced to act before I was fully ready, but I didn't see why I should share my doubts with Russell.

"If you think of trying to make an attempt to escape, then understand this. I may have been chatting amiably to you but that, frankly, was to put you off guard – and it seems to have worked. But if you think you deserve any charity from me, think again. Just reflect that you mugged me, beat me up, and have now hijacked me in my own vehicle. You have injected me with drugs against my will. You arranged for Miss Crawford to be kidnapped, bound and imprisoned, and threatened to mutilate her if your wishes were not complied with. We are only two of the people who have reason to withhold any feelings of sympathy for you, but I have no doubt there are very many more."

"Don't, therefore, be surprised if I am not prepared to do you any favours."

The whole of my bitterness towards him flowed out.

"One further point. You think your disc is unreadable. Wrong. The police have a complete copy which they are at this moment using to compile a case against you which will break up your entire organisation. I was flattered that you should ask me to join your outfit, but I am sure that you, now realising what I know, can understand why I did not show immediate interest."

The expressions on his face moved through disbelief, rage, fear and desperation.

He made as if to move, but a sharp tug on the flex reduced him to subservience. I decided to occupy the time until Uncle Jim arrived with some more home truths.

"Do you have any idea why I wouldn't join you now, next week, or ever? Perhaps you wonder why Linus should have attempted to betray you. Well, it was because you betrayed him first. Not only did you introduce his father to the drugs that killed him, but you then tried to use this disreputable knowledge to blackmail an honourable man into doing your dirty work. How can you pretend that you are just 'supplying a demand'?"

"You are creating a demand which you then exploit at other people's cost."

"I don't suppose you even know Steve Whitman. He's probably too insignificant for you to come into contact with. He's a young lad, and a bright one, who you are now forcing to ever greater levels of pushing. He drifted into addiction because he didn't know the risks. He is on the brink of self-destruction. What effect do you think your demands have on him, his family and friends? Do you think it is his fault – or is it yours?"

I realised this was beginning to sound like a Sunday school sermon, but I was certainly engaging his full attention. I had been taking occasional glances out of the window to see if my rescuers were at hand, but had seen nothing. I needed to go on.

I thought I had better shift to a more personal theme. I looked at him. He seemed to have an increasingly contemptuous look on his face. I tugged the flex, and the look disappeared.

"You seem to see yourself as some sort of loveable and gentlemanly rascal who is merely ignoring oppressive laws to give people what they want."

"You're contemptible. You serve nothing but your own greed. You have no concern for other people, but just use them or abuse them in any way that you think suits your purpose.

"Do you really want to know why I was determined to bring you down? The thing that clinched it was the threat you used against Miss Crawford. She had nothing to do with any of this, except indirectly, and yet you chose to make a totally barbaric threat against her. Did you bother to find out what her involvement was? No. Did you ever consider that I might never have had the disc originally, and didn't know where it was? No. She didn't have the disc, and I didn't know anything at all about it. It was by sheer chance that I was able to track it down. If I had failed to find it, you were quite prepared to have her maimed; at least, I can't imagine you would do your own dirty work, but force one of your thugs to do it."

"And you wonder why I decided to smash your racket once and for all."

He looked contemptuously at me, and would have attempted to justify his position if I had not given the flex a sharp tug, nearly choking him. It was just as well he couldn't say anything, because if he had tried to excuse himself I should probably have pulled the flex tighter and held it there.

I glanced once more out of the window, and was absolutely delighted to see one of Uncle Jim's men leading a handcuffed figure away from the house.

I felt nearly as high as I had done on the cocaine. I went over to the door and unlocked it. Then I returned to my seat and moved in for the kill.

"You have been to a lot of trouble to get that disc. Well, cheer up. Here it is."

I took the disc out of my left hand jacket pocket and tossed it on the table.

He couldn't help himself. He took his hands off the table and grabbed the case. He opened it with trembling fingers, and stared at it, verifying its authenticity. He looked at me, mystified, not understanding what was happening.

The door opened, and Uncle Jim appeared.

"Russell Sinclair Deverell, I am arresting you under the 1971 Misuse of Drugs Act." He recited the statutory formula. He turned to me.

"Hello, Oliver, everything OK?"

"Fine," I replied lightly. "Glad you could look in. I know Russell is a bit tied up at the moment, but I think he has something for you."

Uncle Jim produced a handkerchief and placed the disc which Russell had been fingering into a plastic bag, and gave it to one of the men who had followed him into the room.

"Excellent," he said. "That just about puts the tin lid on it. Well done."

Uncle Jim handcuffed Russell and I undid the flex round his neck. We moved the desk away from the wall, and Russell was frogmarched out into the hall.

As he passed me he spoke.

"Bastard! You bastard! You sanctimonious, devious, snide bastard!"

"Thank you so much. That was charmingly put. I obviously have qualities that appeal to you." I couldn't help needling him after what he had put me through.

We followed him out of the room, and there was Nathan, handcuffed, sheepish and resigned. He didn't actually say, 'It's a fair cop, Guv' but he certainly looked it. Perhaps he was thinking what the kidnapping of Emma was going to look like on his record.

There was a police van outside, and Russell and Nathan joined three of his men who were already inside. The van departed.

I made a hurried tour of the place with Uncle Jim, who wanted to collect as much evidence as he could. There was some urgency about this, because it was known that there were other members of the syndicate who would be anxious to destroy any incriminating material if they had the chance, once they realised that Russell had been arrested.

It was fortunate that the van into which Nathan had been loading the office equipment was still there, including three computers. I was able to describe fairly accurately what they were used for, and one of Uncle Jim's men made the necessary notes before driving it away. I pointed out the gun, and Uncle Jim took it so that ballistics and forensic could check if it had any record. He doubted it would, but it was worth a try.

At last we had done as much as we felt we could, and a police cordon was placed round the house, which was for the moment regarded as a scene of crime.

"I'm glad you came when you did," I said as we assembled before departure.

Uncle Jim smiled.

"You seemed to be managing pretty well. Of course, we were able to get a trace on the house, but it took a little longer than we would have liked. You seemed to have everything remarkably under control."

"I was lucky. I don't know what would have happened if Nathan had realised I had jumped his master and come in to see. As it was, I had to keep Russell talking. I was bluffing half the time."

"Remind me not to play poker with you," he said kindly.

"By the way, we retrieved these." He handed me the van keys. "That is partly what took us some time. We didn't know the exact address, because it was not from a house phone but from your mobile. There were several houses that it could have been, and we didn't want to make a mistake. So we surreptitiously looked for your vehicle, since we knew you had been kidnapped in it. The cunning sod had garaged it up, but we found it eventually."

I took my keys gratefully.

"We also retrieved this." He handed me my mobile.

He looked at me knowingly. "She knows you are OK, but I have a feeling that a call from you would be appreciated."

I really liked Uncle Jim.

I pressed the last number redial button, and had a brief but wholly satisfactory conversation with Emma. I then said goodbye to Uncle Jim, got into the van, and drove down the hill to meet Emma where I had agreed – in my flat.

I looked at my watch. It had just gone four.

Chapter 20

The following Saturday I drove over to Emma's flat for lunch. I was still finding it hard to put in perspective all that had happened in the last ten days.

Our reunion the previous Sunday had been an emotional affair. This was partly due to the sudden release of tension which we realised we both had experienced, and partly to the profound sense of relief that we were both now safe from further threat. Having just found each other, the thought of the other being in danger was intolerable.

Emma had returned to her flat. I was absolutely exhausted and slept for sixteen hours. When I woke up it was late Monday morning.

Though I still felt drained, I went in to Mobility and first of all gave James Carwadine a quick version of what had happened. Emma and Linus also came in, but I think we all still looked somewhat shell-shocked so James insisted we should take the day off to recover fully, for which we were all duly grateful.

I had a meal with Emma after work on Wednesday, since the following day would be her last with our firm, and we just needed to see each other by ourselves. We finished up at my flat; and she had invited me over to her place at the weekend.

Over lunch, our conversation inevitably revolved round the events of the previous weekend.

"I was afraid the exchange in Egypt Mill would go wrong," Emma said accusingly. "I don't know why. It just seemed too easy."

"Feminine intuition," I said. "You were quite right."

Well, she had been right, but seemed pleased that I acknowledged it.

"You have no idea what I felt when you didn't return after going back to your flat," she continued. "Ten minutes passed, and then time just dragged by. I could hardly bear it, guessing that you had somehow been taken. We became more and more concerned, and though Uncle Jim suggested that you might have been held up in a traffic accident or something, I didn't believe it. You would have rung. It became more and more obvious that something awful had happened and we knew that you had the disc. Anything could have happened. Russell might just have taken it and killed you."

There were tears in her eyes. I held her even more tightly.

"It was the not knowing anything I found so hard to take," she continued after a moment. "It was like Chinese water torture, every tick of the clock acting like a drop of water."

A shudder convulsed her as she recalled the occasion.

"Please don't do anything like that again. I don't think I could stand it."

I put both my arms round her for a moment before settling back again.

"I didn't really have a choice. You don't, with a gun stuck against your neck. Looking back, I don't suppose he would have used it. I would have been no use to him dead."

"No," she said reflectively, "and you wouldn't have been much use to me dead, either. I would much, much rather have you alive."

I thought it was time to change the subject.

"Anyway, it's good news about Linus. I gather there is no question of any action being taken against him, and both James and Uncle Jim have congratulated him on collecting the vital evidence. It will have no effect on Mobilicity when that one account has been closed, and James says anything that achieves such a useful public service should be applauded, especially as it affected one of his staff. I don't know what is happening about Steve, yet, but Gary is very relieved to know that his brother has a chance to get off the drugs racket altogether."

"Oh, yes," said Emma, "I forgot. Uncle Jim might drop in today. I told him you would be here, so he might have some news. He likes you, by the way."

I was glad to be assured of his approval, especially as I had hopes of joining his family before long.

"I can't get over Russell injecting you" she reflected. "How could he? In cold blood?"

"Yes, he did, and he could. The man has no scruples at all."

"What was it like?" she demanded, requiring a fuller account than I had been able to give her on Wednesday.

I explained the effects it had had on me, and even told her that I could see the attraction – but only for saddos or no-hopers. I had clearly decided that my association with the drugs scene, brief though it had been, confirmed my conviction that it was not for me.

"To think that he could have done that to you – and gone on doing it if he didn't get his way. It makes my blood run cold." She shook her head in disbelief.

"At least I had the chance to tell him what I thought about him. I don't suppose it did any good, but at least it kept him from thinking of ways to turn the tables – and it made me feel better. He even asked me if I wanted a job with him. The sheer cheek of the man, I'd rather go into partnership with a rattlesnake."

"How about a nearly-qualified accountant?" she asked innocently.

"Well, I'd have to think about that." I gave the briefest of pauses. "After due consideration, I think it would be much preferable. Do you know where I can find one?"

She threw a lump of sugar at me. I ducked and she missed. I'm not sure what would have happened next if there had not been a ring on the doorbell, and Uncle Jim appeared. He joined us in an after-lunch coffee.

"You two seem to be getting along well," he remarked, amused, while I picked up the sugar lump. We became a little more serious.

"Well," he said in response to our urgent enquiries, "things are moving fast. Thanks to Linus, the whole fabric of Russell's operation has been exposed. We have already charged Russell, as you saw last Sunday – but that was only because we had sufficient evidence from that disc."

"It was particularly valuable to have caught him in possession. Since he had it on him when he was arrested, with his prints all over it, he cannot deny ownership. Without it, he could well have tried to pretend he knew nothing about it, and a sharp lawyer might have at least got him out on bail. As it is, he was brought before the magistrates on Tuesday, and bail was refused. We're all delighted, because he has the means to escape any time he wants unless he is behind bars. This way, he won't get the opportunity.

"As it is, he will still have access to the best defence lawyers, and may even claim that he had suffered police entrapment."

"You must be joking," I said, astonished "entrapment?"

"Oh, you'll be surprised what they'll try," Uncle Jim replied grimly. "Anything that can be made to look as though the police acted unfairly is often used to try to win sympathy from a jury. I just hope they try it in this case. We will be able to bring in the whole matter of his kidnapping of Emma, and the threat to her fingers. If they do that, you can imagine what effect it would have on any jury; and the press will have a field day. I presume both of you will be prepared to give evidence, if it is necessary?"

"Certainly". Emma and I spoke as one.

"Excellent. I knew you would. It might be that you will have to run the gamut of press coverage, and be dubbed 'Have-a-go heroes' or 'Hostage heroine' or some such drivel, but I suspect Russell's 'Privileged Life of Vice' will be thought to sell more papers. It usually does, unless there is a love angle to it."

He looked non-committally at us, and Emma blushed. I may have gone a bit pink myself. Neither of us wished to make any comment at the time. We hadn't gone far enough to go public yet, and I suspect Uncle Jim was just preparing us for what we might have to expect from the press if the situation arose. He wasn't a fool. I decided to change the subject.

"What about Steve Whitman?" I wanted to know. His position had been bothering me as much as anything. "Will he be charged for his pushing activities?"

"Ah yes," said Uncle Jim, suddenly serious. "I can say to you that, officially, we have no evidence that he has been involved in any illegal practices. There may be hearsay evidence, but this can hardly be substantiated."

"In any case, with someone so comparatively young, seeing it would be a first offence, he would almost certainly not be sent to gaol, but placed on a rehabilitation course. Now I understand that an anonymous donor has offered a sum of money that should more than cover the cost of an effective treatment, but might also leave enough for him to complete his studies and set himself up properly. I'm sure that would be the best solution all round. I have spoken to the lad at length, and I have no doubt that he wants to kick the habit."

I was delighted.

"So Linus came up with the money?" I queried.

Uncle Jim looked puzzled.

"Linus? Money? I've no idea what you are talking about."

Emma opened her mouth to ask a question; but she looked at Uncle Jim, and then at me, and decided against it.

There are some things that are better not pursued officially. We all understood each other perfectly.

"Does Gary know about this? He's really cut up about his brother."

"Yes, he does know. I spoke to him yesterday, as soon as the details had been sorted out. He was, as he put it, externally ingratiated."

We all laughed.

"Good old Gary. I bet he was. I'm so glad. I just feel he deserves a break."

Uncle Jim delivered his final bit of information.

"There is another piece of good news. Linus has given us the details of the special account, and it has been frozen. Russell and his cronies have no access to it, and there is a very good chance that the whole lot will be impounded as the proceeds of crime. With any luck, they will never see a penny of it."

We chatted for a few more minutes, and though I enjoyed his company, he seemed to feel that we might like some time to ourselves.

As I said, he was no fool.

We cleared away our lunch things, and settled down comfortably on Emma's sofa.

"Just think," I mused. "A hell of a lot seems to have happened since a week ago last Thursday. We've both been kidnapped, we've both been threatened with dire retribution, I could have been started on the life of a drug addict, and we've both played our part in smashing a particularly vicious drug racket."

"It was all a bit hairy at the time, but I think we achieved a good result. But do you know what the best thing about all this is?"

"Tell me."

"Finding you. I hope I never lose you again." I kissed her.

"We certainly seem to get on," she said dreamily. "Shall we eat in tonight?"

"Yes. I'd like that."

"So would I. Did you bring any more of that Pouilly-Whatsit?"

"Yes, several bottles. Why?"

"Well, it seemed to work very well last time. That was when we found out just how well we hit it off"

I kissed her. "Talking of hitting it off, I thoroughly enjoyed our conversation when I rang you with Russell's demands. You were fantastic, once you twigged."

She stirred. "It was all very well, but I was anxious about you. Then you chatted on as though there was nothing the matter. Are you surprised I didn't twig at first?"

"I had great faith in you and you understood."

"Okay, I knew you had the disc, so there must be some other reason you were telling me to produce it. Then you asked if there was enough time, and by then Uncle Jim was getting a bearing on your position. He had been expecting you to call. He could have pinpointed the exact house if it had been one of Russell's house phones, but at least we could draw a line on the map along which you would be.

"Then you did the bit about nipping across to the shop for a rum and raisin ice cream. Well, I was just glad we had mentioned it the other night."

"So was I," I said with feeling. "It was the only way I could think of to indicate where you should look."

"Of course, I knew at once that you were somewhere in that private development and we could whittle it down to one of three houses. Uncle Jim was off like a shot, but I believe finding your van took longer than he had hoped."

"I wanted to keep you talking as long as possible because I thought you might be trying to get a fix and it might help."

"I realised that. That's why I did the stupid female bit."

"My darling girl – female, certainly: stupid, never," I said with feeling. "You picked up my patronising babble without turning a hair.

Russell seemed to think that was the normal way to talk to girlfriends. I hope you didn't think for a moment I meant it."

"No. It didn't sound like you, and by that time I had realised what you were doing. Uncle Jim was making 'keep it going' signs to me, and I began to enjoy it."

"Emma, you were brilliant. It was because of you that I was able to go through with it all. I was sure you had understood everything, and you had. It gave me confidence. Without that, I would have had to give him back his disc, and he would have no doubt disappeared. As it is, we've got him.

"That's why I thought then and there that you deserved a *seriously* big kiss."

"But you thought that last Sunday."

"Yes."

"And last Wednesday."

"Yes," I said "and I've just thought it again."

The End